# LOVING MEMORIES

## IMOGENE NIX

Print ISBN 9780648484189

*This book is dedicated to any woman who's plus-sized and ever questioned her worth. Just remember, you're beautiful!*

# BLURB

A second chance at love could come with a killer price tag.

Jenny Douglas has the grim task of returning her friend's body to the man she loved.

Steve Davies is grieving for the woman he lost while trying to care for the foster child she left behind—a little girl he has come to think of as his own.

Jenny and Steve must work together to try to figure out who killed Cara. And if a little bit of passion gets in the way, well...it's not the real thing...or is it?

Content Warning: contains sexual content and mental health issues that some may find confronting

# PROLOGUE

The room was dark and the air cool. Cara's body throbbed as the puddle of blood beneath her grew larger.

"Why? Why did he do this?" Her voice sounded thin, and she swiped her tongue over her cracked lips. It wasn't meant to end this way. He'd smashed the phone, and taken her cell, so she couldn't call for help. Ensuring she wouldn't be found alive.

The knowledge that they'd find out the things she'd done sat in the forefront of her mind. Everything she'd achieved would fall apart once she was gone. Dammit. She'd worked so hard to plan for all the most important things and had missed this—that one person would betray her.

She'd used this trip to Melbourne as a blind. She'd told Steve she was coming to visit Jenny. Clearly, she'd miscalculated badly. Now her plans were shattered because she hadn't considered betrayal.

Once she was gone, Jenny and Steve would forget her—her legacy incomplete and lost. "No. I won't let them forget me."

A sound left her quaking. He might come back. Then it would be too late.

*What to do?* A note. If she left them a note, maybe it would muddy things enough that they would remember her fondly. A seed of regret for past actions bloomed.

With shaking hands, Cara dragged herself toward the bed. She knew there'd be a pen in her bag, and maybe she could find something to write on. Pulling herself up stole the breath in her body. Winded, she lay half-on, half-off the bed.

Her body was cooling, the extremities tingling now. Her eyes sought a flash of white and found a receipt stuffed into the side of her handbag. It would work. She dragged her bag closer and reached inside. The movement hurt, and a low moan escaped her lips.

Cara panted, her energy now melting away.

Her fingers clutched the pen, the tiny gold one that Steve had bought her, and she started to write. Laboriously, but when it was done, she slumped to the bed. Time passed and the light in the room grew dim.

Another sound impinged on her. Hide it. Hide the letter. No one must find it, at least not until the police come. She accepted now it was all over. She was going to die here in this dingy, little room. Alone.

# CHAPTER ONE

The knock at the door at seven AM while Jenny was getting ready for work startled her.

"Hang on!" she called.

She hurried down the hallway from the kitchen and grasped the brass handle. As she tugged the door open, she saw a policeman. She couldn't miss the stiffness of his stance, and the marked car on the road behind him had her gut churning.

"Miss Douglas? I'm Detective Inspector Reid. We've traced you via the police database as an emergency contact for Cara Stewart. Is that correct?"

"Yes, I'm all the family she has. Has something happened to Cara? Is she all right? Has she been in an accident?"

"I'm afraid I have bad news. May I come in, please?"

Cold seeped into her pores at his words. Her brain struggled to compute what was happening. "Uh...sure." She led him down the hallway into the kitchen. "Please, sit down," she said, pulling out a chair for herself.

"Cara...she's a close friend?"

"We're like sisters." Jenny couldn't say why, but she knew

instantly. She slumped into her seat, pain searing her insides. "What happened?" she asked, her words strained.

"She passed away sometime yesterday. The circumstances are suspicious, so we need to investigate it. I'm sorry for your loss."

She laughed then, a snotty, wet warble. It seemed incongruous that here was a policeman, using the same terminology she always heard in the criminal investigation television shows.

The next hour passed in a blur. Detective Inspector Reid was kind. He offered her support and promised to keep her informed of the status of the investigation. Then he made arrangements for her to take responsibility for Cara—her remains, at least—and her worldly goods.

As Jenny left the morgue, the grim task of identifying Cara's body completed, the
detective stood outside waiting for her.

"Miss Douglas. You're finished?"

The lump in her throat stopped any ability to speak, so she nodded, her hair billowing around her head, and she could see the wild, wispy tendrils in her peripheral vision.

"Once we're done, I can release her effects to you."

It all sounded so impersonal. So final. Her heart pounded, but she refused to look up, not wanting him to see the depths of her pain.

"If you'd step in here." He indicated to a tiny alcove that she hadn't noticed. Her mind whirred, the miasma of grief settling over her in a heavy cloud. It was unbearable right now to even think; if she did, she would remember why she was here, in this horribly soulless place.

"Of course." Breathe through this, Jenny. This part will be over soon.

The vision of Cara on the cold, metal table choked her. The scent —sickly sweet masked by heavy cleaning solutions—still remained in her nostrils. Decay and death, the vile aroma seemed to waft around her even though she was in the offices and far away from the cold rooms where they viewed the deceased. For a moment, Jenny was sure she'd vomit.

"Take a shallow breath. I promise it will pass." Detective Reid laid a gentle hand on her shoulder, reassuring her.

"Thank you. You're very kind." She ducked her head, seeking some inner strength.

"I need you to sign for her items." The officer pushed an official-looking document to her, and she scribbled her signature on the page.

When Jenny raised her head, the detective lifted a clear, plastic bag. Inside were articles of clothing, the deep red tones of dried blood visible. Jenny shuddered.

"Is this all, Detective?"

He shook his head. "No, there's more. Her purse contained four hundred and fifty dollars and thirty-five cents. Credit cards, etcetera. We also have several articles of jewelry—three rings, one set of diamond earrings, a watch, and a necklace."

Jenny looked at him, but for some odd reason, she got the impression there was something more—something he wanted to say but couldn't—and she wondered what it was.

"But what else, Detective?" She hated the thickness of her voice.

"There was one other thing. A letter." He reached into his pocket, producing a small manila envelope.

She reached out, her fingers brushing over the paper. Vertigo assailed, the floor undulating beneath her straining eyes. Were these the last words Cara had written? She broke the seal and slid the paper out.

"It's a photocopy. The original is evidence, but I thought..." His voice died away, and hot tears scalded her eyes.

"It's very kind of you to do this."

"She'd hidden it. Stuffed it down her bra, where no one would find it until she arrived in the morgue. It was clear then that she'd written it after the attack and before she died." Jenny's stomach lurched.

THE PLANE TAXIED TO A STOP, AND AS SOON AS THE SEATBELT light went off, Jenny stood to retrieve her bag from the overhead compartment. Here she was, back home in Brisbane. The damned anger and sadness still blocked her throat. She cleared it, rubbed her hands across her eyes, and started to work her way up the aisle toward the exit.

As she left the plane, the attendants gave her their politely disinterested 'we know you still have a long, sad trip ahead of you' smiles. She trudged up the empty corridor into the airport terminal. Jenny had arranged for the funeral home to meet the plane and retrieve the coffin. It had been very hard flying from Melbourne to Brisbane knowing Cara was below her in the hold in a casket. This would be the last trip Cara ever made.

Jenny's carry-on bag weighed her down as she reached the baggage claim area. The intercom ran continual notices, and she scanned the bags, searching for hers and Cara's, ignoring the happy people crowding around her. Finally, her backpack and Cara's expensive Gucci suitcase, which Jenny had tied yellow ribbons to, came into view. She moved forward, snagging them both before retreating from the knots of carefree travelers. She dragged them to the trolleys, slipped a coin into the release, and placed the heavy bags onto it before heading toward the door.

The intercom made a ding-dong noise again. "Paging Miss Jenny Douglas. Jenny Douglas. If you're in the terminal, please make your way to the information desk."

"Oh God, what on earth's wrong now?" She muttered the words as she turned and pushed the trolley toward the designated area.

In front of the desk stood a gorgeous, tall, muscular man with black hair curling at his neck to caress his nape. The woman manning the desk spoke quietly, her hand patting the man's as if soothing some deep emotion. His face was tight and drawn, as if he were enduring some hidden pain.

Holding his hand was a tiny, young Eurasian girl. Jenny guessed her to be about five or six years old. An alarm rang in her brain.

Was this Steve? Who was the little girl beside him, and why couldn't she pull her gaze away from them? She clenched her fingers around the handle of the baggage cart and inhaled deeply, seeking to balance herself emotionally before stepping in his direction. The jitters that ran like a fine current of electricity through her eased somewhat. She hadn't expected to see him. Their arrangements had been that she'd let him know when she arrived in Brisbane. His gaze tracked her as she wheeled the squeaky cart in his direction.

Once she arrived in front of the desk, she glanced at the woman. "I'm Jenny Douglas. You paged me?"

"Miss Douglas, I asked them to page you," said the dark-haired man, stepping forward. "Steve...Steve Davies." His voice carried harshness, as if he had to force the words from his throat. In his eyes, Jenny saw the grief and loss, along with the white lines of pain that flanked his lips.

Jenny knew his name. She'd seen it written on the crumpled paper in her pocket. Her eyes stung and watered again even as she told herself sternly that any attraction she felt was wrong. He was Cara's man. The relationship between them was clear in the letter Cara had left for her.

"Hi, Steve." She held out her hand, and he shook it in three firm movements. The little girl squeezed in against the big man's side, the movement catching her attention. Jenny glanced down at the young girl who wound an arm around Steve's leg. "Hi."

The girl blinked but remained silent, and Jenny quickly realized that the little girl wasn't very trusting. That was evident by the way she gripped tighter and seemed to shrink into the man she clung to.

Jenny looked back at the man in front of her, and the bubbly sensation, as if a million tiny bugs were flying around, started in her gut. As the feeling rose, she firmly stamped it out.

"I, umm... Have you got transportation organized?" His eyes reflected pain, as if it were too great a burden to carry, but his spine remained stiff, cradling the child close. "The undertaker's email said you were coming in on this flight and the... Cara..." He stopped, and she took pity on him.

"Yes, Cara's casket is being met by the undertaker. I was going to grab a taxi..." She stopped short as he shook his head. "Does..." She nodded to the child, wondering not for the first time if the girl was aware of what was happening.

He inclined his head, indicating that the little girl knew about Cara. "We'll take you. Where are you staying?"

Jenny named her hotel, and he grimaced.

"It's a bit...run down."

She shrugged. This trip alone was a stretch financially, but she couldn't...wouldn't do anything less for Cara.

He nodded, and for an instant, she wondered what he had thought when he'd first seen her, then she shook herself. He was grieving for Cara, and she was a fool. A size eighteen fool at that.

"Can we...go?" Jenny spoke quietly. Right now she needed silence, the noise and bustle of the airport too much for her mind to process.

Steve released the girl and held out a hand, which the child took. "Come on, Lola. Let's take Jenny to the car, okay?"

She waited for him to lead the way, the little girl clinging to his hand. The child hadn't said a word, just watched Jenny through lost, empty eyes. Time and time again in her profession as a psychologist, Jenny had seen that same look from those who'd lost someone close.

They left the terminal, making their way through the maze of concrete works to the large multi-storied car park as loud and impersonal as any other. He moved unerringly toward a new model sedan, stopped, and clicked the button on the remote control. The turn signal lamps flashed accompanied by a beep of the horn. The girl he called Lola let go of his hand and climbed into the vehicle.

She glanced at the child, the psychologist inside her wondering what she could say to help with the pain the young girl must be feeling. But the broken woman inside her wanted to keep a distance, so she kept quiet.

Once the bags were stowed she pushed the cart to a nearby return bay and pocketed the change, then made her way to the car and climbed in. The engine roared to life and she settled back into the comfortable leather seat, pulling on her seatbelt. He drove slowly past the bay of cars.

The silence grew uncomfortable, and she asked quietly, "Have you known Cara for long?"

He glanced at her then looked away. She hadn't even known about him until the letter from Cara was placed in her hand. The knowledge that Cara was in a long-term relationship but had never told her had scored her at first. Then she'd reminded herself that they were living different and separate lives. Besides, Cara would have told her about him at some point soon. Now though, Jenny felt a determination to understand his importance in Cara's life.

"I met her several months ago." His terse, arctic tone stopped her questions and ended the conversation. Jenny turned away.

How can I sort through the jumbled mess Cara left me if I can't even get an answer from him? Her fingers sought and found the letter once more in her pocket where she had hidden it. She ran a shaking fingertip along the edges of a crease line. She didn't need to read it again to know the contents. They were burned into her memory. She'd have to share it soon, but not yet.

At this moment in time she wished she could forget it and the information it contained, but its existence was like picking at a scab, her mind returning to it, and the pain reminded her that she was here and this was her reality. Her mind helpfully supplied a vision of the paper, the dark smears of blood that had coated it, and the ever-present nausea rose.

It was all too much for her to contemplate right now, and the view from the car window blurred.

"Jenny, I'm sorry."

She closed her eyes at the choked sound of Steve's voice. It seemed unfair that this big, strong man was reduced to...what? Misery? She wanted to tell him that went with the territory of dealing with someone who'd been murdered. But instead she tensed her jaw, holding in the thoughts as they drove along. It would only wound him, and they both carried enough wounds already.

She tugged on the sleeves of her shirt, hiding the reminders of her own.

Steve finally slowed the car and turned into a small hotel. It was ugly and dirty. Seedy with an air of desperation hanging about it. It might have been the refuse and over-filled bins, it could have been the greasy entrance or those loitering by the door, but everything together reinforced her concern. Jenny's stomach knotted further. Why had she picked this place? Even online it had looked downtrodden. Now that she was here, it was worse. Several older cars, rusted and dented, sat in the parking lot, and the buildings around were shuttered with dirty, metal grates. She gulped her dismay.

"Are you sure you want to stay here?" His tone questioned her judgment, and she looked

at the ugly, dirty façade, questioning the sanity of remaining here.

It's the best you can afford, she thought, but her very soul recoiled at that reality. "I... Uh,

I have a booking for this hotel." The stink that rose turned her already fragile stomach. She'd have to make the best of it, because anything else was beyond her ability to pay. She still had long-standing bills from her psychology degree that hung over her head. Jenny gifted Steve with her practiced smile, hand on the door as she prepared to open it. "It can't be that bad...can it?"

He grunted in reply and opened his car door as she did the same on her side. Lola climbed out after her and watched Jenny with passive brown eyes.

"We can leave your stuff here until you check in." His gruff voice told her he didn't expect her to stay, but she shrugged her heavy carry-on bag over her shoulder. The beep of the central locking left her frowning, and they wandered to the dirty doors of the hotel.

The smell of stale urine and something else entered her nostrils as soon as she opened the door. It reinforced her misgivings, but it was the drunk in the corner of the lobby that stopped her in her tracks.

"You're not staying here." Steve's voice broke her horrified trance, and he pulled her back out the door. "You can come home with me."

"I don't..."

"Look. I owe you. For Cara. Please?"

Misgivings rose, but in that split second, her mind was made up. If she stayed at his place, she would feel a lot more secure while finishing what she came to achieve. She wouldn't need to split her focus between worrying about her belongings and dealing with Cara's requirements. She bit her lip, a tiny seed of concern rising, but she thrust it aside. For Cara. "Okay. I'll stay with you."

He gave a short, sharp nod and propelled her back to the car. Once more settled within, she looked out the window as they drove away.

Steve had noticed the woman when she entered the baggage claim area. Her long, black hair had moved slowly in time with the sensuous movements of her body as she walked toward the carousel. He had been struck by her innate grace and generous curves. *Cara. I have to remember Cara.* That didn't stop his body reacting though, unconsciously longing for something forbidden.

Anger rose like a black cloud, filling him. Things hadn't been perfect between him and Cara, but he'd loved her. The desperation in his thoughts increased the sensation of guilt that tugged at him.

After the last of the baggage had been claimed he'd asked the person at the information desk to make the announcement, his surprise palpable as the black-haired woman had pushed her cart over to where he and Lola had waited. The woman's green eyes were filled with sadness.

Steve couldn't help the conflicting emotions that filled him. He was grateful she'd stayed with Cara on her final journey home, but he wished this Jenny Douglas far away.

His fingers tightened around the leather cover of the steering wheel. He had stunned himself when he offered to take her to the hotel. His memories of it, the prostitutes who frequented it, and of course, the drug dealers who loitered on the corners, selling their wares, had turned him icy cold. He told himself it was only because she'd been so loyal to Cara that he cared. His conscience remained quiet on that front.

"You said you found my contact information..." Steve spoke quietly, hoping she'd fill in the blanks.

"On Cara's computer. She was nothing if not predictable. Always kept the same password, so it was easy to access her files and find your details."

"Yes. So you said."

That Cara was gone still seemed inconceivable. Jenny had rung him, after finding his contact details, and broken the news. He didn't want to relive that experience, the cold that had washed over him, the dread. The relief...

Steve shied away from considering what that meant. He'd loved Cara.

He eased the car around the corner, thinking over Jenny's assertions that she'd stay here at the King's Arms hotel. He'd heard the determination in her voice and shrugged, knowing that if she was in any form of right mind, when she entered the shabby foyer, she'd change her mind.

In the end, all it had taken was a single drunk in the corner and the smell of stale urine to bring her to a standstill. Funny, he would have thought the visage that presented at the front door would have done the trick. He grabbed her hand, made his offer, then towed her back to the car, watching as Lola climbed in.

Jenny turned, her face drawn and white. Her green eyes luminous orbs of misery. "You were right, I couldn't stay there. Thanks for saving me."

He laughed, not much more than a short bark, but it was more than he'd managed since receiving the news about Cara. Heading for the driver's side door, he slipped into the seat. Jenny had already pulled on her seatbelt, and he did the same.

He noted the flicker of her gaze, one that encompassed the seedy neighborhood. They needed to get back on the road as soon as possible. The car purred as he fired the ignition and indicated before pulling into the flow of traffic. Just in time, he thought as two dark figures emerged from the shadows where the car had been parked.

The tires hummed as they drove, and he chanced a look at Jenny, her eyes averted in the direction of the window. Once more in an established neighborhood, flickers of scrubby trees and old wooden fences filled the glass, and he sighed. He'd been short with her before. Steve hurriedly looked back to the road, catching sight of Lola's gaze in the mirror. He smiled at the little girl, and she gave him a half-smile that had almost become her signature.

If only she'd talk.

He'd met Cara through Lola. Cara had found the girl foraging through the garbage outside her unit and taken her in, fed her, and even bought her some clothes to replace the rags she'd been wearing. Lola hadn't spoken a word since that day.

Cara had contacted the police, seeking assistance to identify the child and where she'd come from. Those questions had never been answered, and Steve still didn't know where or who her parents were.

He and his partner, Dave, had answered the call that fateful day. All it took was one look from Cara and he was lost. It wasn't her big breasts or doe brown eyes that hooked him, nor was it her long, blonde hair. It was her smile, her laugh, and how she'd been so alive. The effervescent nature that bubbled with laughter and her flirtatious wit had drugged him. Cara... Now she was gone, her light snuffed out, and he couldn't comprehend how the world could continue without her in it.

Jenny turned toward him, and he cleared his throat, willing away the sudden sheen of moisture that filled his vision.

"Uh, Steve?"

"It's nothing." It wasn't, but right now he couldn't bring himself to say anything. Instead, he pondered how this could have happened. He knew that the police in Victoria thought it was a mugging gone wrong. "Detective Reid—he seemed insightful."

"I, uh... I guess so." Her words were faint and clearly dismissive. "Your daughter is lovely."

He sputtered with surprise, then sighed. It would be an easy mistake to make, he guessed. "She's not actually my daughter. Well, she sort of is. It's a long story."

With a shrug, Jenny gazed back at the window, setting up an emotional barrier, and his thoughts returned to Lola.

He'd been aware immediately of Cara's desire to help Lola. He'd been more than happy to do what he could in his spare time. Then someone had sent Cara threatening notes and things had escalated.

"Cara never really struck me as the parental kind. How did she... I mean, how did Cara deal with Lola?"

He blinked. "She was the main carer, but as we got closer, we kind of split the duties." The sound of surprise she made had him whipping his gaze in her direction. "You seem surprised by that."

"A little. She was never very interested in kids, you know?"

"When she found Lola, she didn't even know her name. Lola was the next name on the worker's assigned name list. Anyway, Cara fought to keep her. Child Services was overstretched, so they agreed to let her stay with Cara in the short term."

"Uh, I'm confused. Cara found her?"

"Something like that, but I'd rather discuss this later." He glanced in the rearview mirror, his gaze connecting with Lola's. She'd had enough to deal with in her short life; she didn't need to listen to people talking about her.

She really didn't know Cara very well if she thought that Cara didn't care for the child, but there'd been a nagging doubt from the beginning. Something that seemed off, even when he'd met Cara. But her concern for Lola was something he'd never questioned.

*His personal cell pealed and he reached over, reading the screen. It was a number he knew all too well—Cara. "Steve Davies speaking."*

*"Oh God! Someone's sent me a note, and they're probably still outside.*

*It's... I can't..."*

*The sound of her breathy voice fired his protective instincts, and his hackles rose instantly.*

*"Are you at home? He shuffled the items around on his desk, looking*

*for his keys and wallet.*

*"She's here with me. Can we... Do you mind if we head to the station?" The wariness in her voice ripped at his guts. "You stay where you are.*

*I'll be right over. Make sure the doors are locked and stay away from the windows. I'll ring your cell when I get to your door. Keep it with you."*

*"Thank... Thank you."*

Once he'd arrived at her apartment, he read the note that described the horrendous things they'd do to them if she didn't hand Lola over. His fury had built, and he'd been unable to let them remain alone. Instead, he'd taken them both to his home. Things had escalated quickly then into a full-blown sexual relationship. One that was firmly against the rules.

Of course, he'd kept working the case; his need to solve the case and keep them safe paramount. Some weeks later his captain had caught him in the corridor.

*"Steve, I understand you have guests." The smile directed at him was heavy with frustration. "You know the rules."*

*"But, sir..."*

*"Either remove yourself from the case, or I'll do it for you. You cannot be emotionally involved with this woman while investigating her case. It's a clear conflict of interest."*

*Anger rippled through him, his nerve endings jumping.*

*The captain pierced him with a stern look, but Steve considered everything he knew. Cara and Lola, or the law. He couldn't continue in charge of the case, and that wasn't acceptable. He needed to protect them, needed to keep them safe and find whoever was making the threats. There was no contest.*

*"Then I'll tender my resignation in writing at the end of the shift."*

*His captain looked stunned. "Steve, don't resign. Take a leave of absence if you must, but don't act in haste."*

Cara had taken Lola home days later, arguing that she needed her space and she wanted Lola to have stability. He hadn't wanted to let her go, but by then, he'd walked away from the police service.

Dave, his best friend, had questioned his sanity when he gave up his career for Cara. He'd spoken his mind in the beginning, but now he kept his mouth firmly closed. He'd been a rock since hearing of Cara's death. For that, Steve remained grateful.

Cara. He'd promised to find whoever was after her. To keep her safe. He grimaced, remembering their last night together, how he'd told her he would lay his own life down for her. She'd laughed and told him he was being melodramatic before kissing him passionately.

That had led to something quite different. His stomach churned as he remembered the intimate encounter, and his eyes burned while his fingers gripped the steering wheel.

*I failed you, Cara, but I promise I will protect Lola.*

She'd left the following morning, after an argument, on a flight to Melbourne. She'd told him she was going to consult with a friend, a psychologist, about Lola.

A shrink. He'd growled when she opened the conversation over dinner that last night. She'd laughed and told him that this one was different. That she cared. Then she'd changed the topic, ensnaring him once again in the passionate web that she always seemed to weave.

The next morning, he'd been angry again, sure that they could heal Lola together. No matter his misgivings though, he'd taken Lola home, just as he'd promised to do the night before.

Now Cara was gone. The woman he had loved for such a short time was snuffed out like a candle flame.

He shook his head as the moisture gathered in his eyes again. He scrubbed a shaking hand over his stubble.

"Almost there," he growled as much to himself as to Jenny.

The exit loomed ahead and he indicated, about to pull in when a dark van pulled alongside and swerved. His brain clicked into hyper-awareness. He knew what was coming before the collision occurred.

"Hold on!" He stomped on the brakes. The car fishtailed, and he used every ounce of his strength pulling it to a stop as his gaze flickered between the rearview mirror and the road ahead.

His heart thudded in his chest. Lola! He started to turn but noticed Jenny had flung an arm out between the two front seats, creating a fragile barrier. Lola grunted as the seatbelt caught her and gripped tight, her eyes wide. It only took a split second for him to take everything in, but limpness invaded his body upon seeing the child and woman unhurt.

"No... No one injured?"

Lola shook her head as Jenny murmured a faint, "No."

"Good. We need to get out of here."

He glanced ahead, in the direction of the offending vehicle. It had sped away and was out of sight, but that didn't mean anything. The longer they stayed there, the more the danger grew. They'd stopped on the verge, two wheels on the grass, and he inhaled deeply, thanking lack of traffic for their safety. His stomach churned. It could have been so much worse.

"She warned me. It was in the letter, I just didn't see it." Jenny's voice filled the silence in the car, and he whipped around, brows drawing together as he looked at her white face.

Doom filled him. "What letter?"

"The one I have in my pocket."

"You never said…"

She had a letter, one that clearly showed there was extreme danger, though why Cara would write a letter to this woman… He wanted to ask more, but didn't. Now wasn't the time. Lola was there, and enough had happened today without her hearing something that might hurt her further. Whatever was in that letter couldn't help anyone right now.

"Let's head home and you can tell me about it once we get there." He couldn't help the terseness of his words.

Even as he considered the situation, another thought bloomed. Jenny seemed somehow broken. As if she were missing an essential part of herself. He couldn't balance his angry thoughts against the protective emotions that rose when he looked at her. It didn't seem right to attack her because Cara had decided she needed to write to her instead of him—but that knowledge burned his guts.

On the other hand, she'd brought more danger with her; danger that Lola didn't need or deserve. He'd get to the bottom of this, and he'd do whatever it took to keep the child safe, even from the woman in the seat beside him.

# CHAPTER TWO

Night had fallen during the drive and exhaustion beat like a tattoo at her mind. Jenny didn't get a look at the house, only noted that it seemed large in the gloom. But then, given that the residence was within a gated community, that also could be assumption.

The garage door opened at the flick of a switch, and Steve drove inside it. Lola let herself out of the car and into the house, turning on light switches as she went. Jenny wearily followed to the doorway then stopped. Steve was reaching for the bags in the boot of the car and dropped the first to the floor with an oomph. Jenny hurried over to help.

"I'll take that." She bent to grab the handle as he dropped the second, their heads connecting painfully. "Ow!" Jenny stepped back quickly, her foot slipping, and she fell to the concrete floor, landing on her backside. "Damn."

Her bum stung and her head ached. Her eyes burned, and to be honest, she just wanted to be alone long enough to sort through her jumbled thoughts. This isn't the way a good guest behaves, she reminded herself. She wobbled slightly as she stood.

"I'm sorry. Do you need a hand?"

Jenny glanced at him. "No. I can do this."

He frowned. "You're sure you're okay?" His eyes flickered over her face, and she could feel the confusion and embarrassment flooding hers with heat.

"Yeah, I'm fine. Do I go through here?" She pointed to the doorway Lola had retreated through, and he nodded. Retrieving the handle, she pulled the bag behind her and listened to the wheels whirr along the floor.

His hand rested on her shoulder and she stilled, feeling a zing of connection. "Bring the bag down here to the guest room."

She looked around and caught sight of his eyes, mesmerizing and deep. Jenny nodded, and he pulled away, leading her to a bedroom.

He opened the door and tsked. "Sorry, I forgot to move the laundry." He dropped the backpack he carried next to the bed.

Bemusement filled her as she noted the baskets of clean clothes and the ironing board with an iron sitting on it.

The room wasn't exactly small, and as she stepped over the doorway she could see the built-in robes and another door.

"That's your en-suite there." He inclined his head to a closed door while grabbing the first basket of un-ironed washing and hoisting it into one side of the wardrobe, then he piled a second basket on top of it. "It's for the ironing lady. Uh, I've never been good with an iron. If you don't mind just using one side of the wardrobe, I can move the rest of this out of your way."

He stepped aside and indicated the old, heavy, wooden drawers against the wall. They carried a dark patina of well-waxed furnishings, while the scent of lemon filled the air and light glinted from the dull, metal handles.

"If you need anything else, you'll find towels, blankets, and stuff in the bottom drawer." He lugged one bag and then the other to the bed. "Get comfortable and then come out when you're ready."

He left the room, closing the door behind him. Jenny opened the first bag, her own, and started pulling out her clothes, shoving them into drawers and the cupboard.

Her thoughts crowded her, tumbling along in her mind, and she wanted...needed...to stay one step ahead of them, because if she didn't, she knew from long experience that she'd feel the negative emotions that could unbalance her.

"Control. Stay in control, Jenny. That'll get you through." She whispered the words to her reflection in the mirror and returned to her task.

Once she had her backpack empty, she opened the door to the en-suite and placed her toiletries on the large, white, marble vanity unit and studied her reflection with a sigh. There really wasn't much she could do with herself. For a moment she toyed with the idea of a shower, but she'd been in there a while and knew she should probably go out and be somewhat social. Not that she really wanted to.

Her gaze took in the black hair that stood up in clumps from running her fingers through it while unpacking. Her eye makeup left her looking like some kind of Goth raccoon, with smudged and smeared mascara.

"You can't go out there looking like that." The firmness in her voice belied the wobble of her chin as emotions welled.

Her gaze settled on the black, ruffled blouse and straight, black pants which she'd thought were at least well-fitting, only to realize that the pants puckered a little along the sides and the blouse revealed a little too much flesh for her size.

Her shoulders slumped. "That's what you get for not looking in the mirror."

The truth was, though, that all she could do was cope from day-to-day right now. If it took refusing to look too closely at her clothing choices, then so be it. The drawback was times like this.

Cara had been a perfect size eight with long, blonde hair and dark brown eyes. She'd been the one all the guys wanted to date and the girls wanted to be friends with. Not the dark- haired, plus-sized girl.

Jenny's gaze fell to the white scars on her wrists. Marks she wished she could forget about, but they were there. Reminders of what she'd felt and how she'd abused her body in the past. Reminders of how far she had come.

No matter how much she tried to hide from the truth though, her weight was only one aspect of her depression and self-esteem issues.

Jenny pulled away from the mirror, knowing if she stayed, the morbid thoughts would catch up with her. It was a coping strategy she'd finally found. One that worked for her. It might not be technically accepted practice to ignore and hide from the truth, but it had proved successful every time she employed it. It had kept her alive when there was little to look forward to.

She hurried back to the bedroom and pushed her bag to the floor before she opened Cara's.

Inside was a wild jumble of clothes. Whatever she'd thought could be achieved by unpacking it—and that path only led to more confusion—would wait. The pain cut deep...too deep right now. Tears burned behind her lids, and she quickly zipped the bag up.

Better to deal with this when she was more settled. Carefully, she lifted the bag and set it on the floor at the end of the bed. Later, she promised herself.

She smoothed down her clothes and finger-brushed her hair. Next Jenny tidied her makeup and inhaled deeply before heading for the door. The corridor was long and cool, and she walked in the direction of Steve's voice. Thuds and taps, along with clunks and crunches filled the air, and she peeked around the corner wall into the kitchen. Lola sat perched on a stool and Steve peeled vegetables in the sink.

"So I'm thinking, tonight we grill some chicken breasts and veggies. Maybe even fruit salad for dessert. What do you say to that, Lola? Think our guest would find that acceptable?" Neither had seen her and she watched as Lola nodded, peeling a carrot. Every now and again it fell from her grip to the dark granite worktop with a thud. Jenny bit her lip, watching for a minute longer, then saw Steve pull away from the sink.

She moved around the corner. "Hi there."

Steve turned, and his small smile warmed her inside. It lit up his face, crinkling the corner of his eyes and his mouth, and hers dried up as a spark of interest suffused her. Control yourself, Jenny. This is Cara's guy. You know...the girl you came to bury? She stopped still as her mind reminded her of the truth. Besides which, after the gorgeous Cara, she was a frumpy cow. The familiar weight of grief and self-doubt settled back on her shoulders.

Jenny moved hesitantly toward Lola. "You're doing an excellent job there. Can I help?"

The child looked at her as if assessing her, and Jenny had the feeling she saw a lot more than she let on. That was usually the way with silent children. Jenny wondered what lay at the heart of it.

"I hope you like grilled chicken and veggies."

Jenny looked up, nodding at Steve's words. "That would be lovely. Can I help?" She moved forward and he shook his head.

"I thought we could eat in here tonight, and then Lola's heading to bed. It's been a long day for her. Then you and I can talk about things."

Jenny knew he was right. They needed to talk. She needed to share the letter. And it would be good to have someone to talk to about Cara—someone who knew Cara as well as, or possibly more so, than she herself did.

"Sure, okay," Jenny replied.

She sat down on a vacant stool and watched as Lola slipped off hers, grabbing some plates, knives, and forks. It was obvious she was quite at home here. She might not be Steve's biological daughter, but there was a close bond between the two.

The sound of meat sizzling on a griddle filled the air, and she salivated at the delicious smells that emanated. Jenny waited as Steve moved around, clearly comfortable in the role of cook. She smiled. It had been a very long time since she'd been in a kitchen filled with such delicious smells.

Steve turned back and smiled. "If you would like a drink, Lola will show you where the glasses are. There's some wine or soda water in the fridge. Cool water comes from the extra tap. Help yourself."

"I'll grab a soda water, thanks." She rose and Lola indicated a high cupboard. She reached up, grabbed two wine glasses, and noted a small plastic cup on the benchtop. "Would you like a drink too, Steve?"

"Yeah, I'll take a soda water too. Could you squeeze a little lime juice into it?"

"Sure." Jenny quickly set about the task of adding some citrus juice to both. Lola grabbed a plastic cup and pointed to the juice, which Jenny poured, then settled back into her seat.

Steve carried the meat and vegetables over, settling in beside her as he placed the hot griddle on a heat stone on the breakfast bar. They helped themselves to the medley of vegetables and chicken, which was perfect and tender. Not for the first time, she felt just a hint of jealousy toward Cara.

Once again she'd got the perfect guy. Then she reminded herself that Cara didn't get the perfect outcome though. After all, wasn't that why she was here? Her stomach bottomed out at the thought.

THE DISHWASHER WAS LOADED AND HUMMING AWAY, AND STEVE had taken Lola down the hall

to settle her into bed. Jenny made her way into the lounge, studying the photos on the walls. There was a large one of a wedding, and she was pretty sure the couple was his parents. The wedding gown was early eighties, the bride's hair big curls, and the wedding party wore pastel suits edged with ruffles. There'd been nothing like these happy images on the walls growing up in her house.

She moved along the wall, seeing a photo of Steve, younger and dressed in his police uniform. It must have been when he finished at the academy. She smiled, wondering if she'd ever looked that young herself. The next one was of him and another man. They were obviously good friends, judging by the way the man stood close by Steve as they both held up a tin of beer, dressed in casual clothes and sporting broad grins. Jenny wondered at the story behind the photo. Was it some kind of special event? A birthday or promotion? She moved on.

Jenny stopped at a photo of him and Cara, arms entwined and faces close together. If she'd needed any proof they had been an item, there it was. The next was of Cara, Steve, and Lola. They smiled out at her like some kind of happy family, and the feeling that she had somehow intruded on precious memories jerked her away from the image.

"That was taken the week before she left." The sound of Steve's voice surprised her, and she turned.

"I'm sorry, I shouldn't have…"

He shook his head. "No, it's fine."

He indicated a bottle of brown spirits. The scent in the air told her it was a well-known Australian rum. She thought for a minute about his offer, then nodded.

Jenny wasn't much of a drinker, rarely indulging in such things, because the consequences could be disastrous if she dipped into a depressive mood. She knew her personal foibles well enough, but tonight, she needed a dash of courage.

Steve poured two healthy splashes of gold liquid into glasses and held one out for her. "Make yourself comfortable. I doubt this is going to be an easy conversation."

"I think you're right about that," she said as she took the glass.

He trailed over to a seat, holding the bottle in one hand and his glass in the other.

Jenny took a sip of the liquid. It burned a path down her throat, and she coughed away the burn.

"Are you okay?"

For a moment she felt the warmth of concern envelop her. She smiled. "Yeah."

He settled into the chair, his feet crossed, while the rum balanced on the arm of the seat, and looked pointedly in her direction. "The letter? You'll tell me about it?"

Jenny nodded and reached into her pocket, drawing the crumpled paper out and unfolding it, smoothing it with shaking fingers. "I'd... If you don't mind, I'll read it out loud. There's some..." She swallowed the last of her drink. "There's some deeply personal stuff in it I don't feel comfortable sharing." She finished the words in a rush and hoped like hell he'd understand.

He nodded but thankfully remained silent.

She glanced down at the copy, noting the way her fingers shook. The paper rustled, and for a moment, her courage fled. It took every ounce of willpower for her to draw another breath, settle the nerves, then begin.

"Uh...so she starts out with:

*Jenny, I don't have a lot of time. By the time you get this, I will be gone. I need you to do a couple of things for me. Take my stuff to Steve Davies. You'll find a link on the last email I sent. Take me back to him. Look after him and Lola, they need help. More than either of them understands right now."*

Jenny stopped, heaving a gulp of air and struggling with the tenuous threads of composure before she continued.

*"If only you'd been here, but you weren't, and I won't get to share with you how fabulous my life is, or was. I don't want to leave. Tell Steve and Lola I wish I was with them. Of course they need to go on, live their lives without me, but ask them to remember me. Full of life and fun, because that's what I was, we both know that. Jenny, remember to always be true to yourself, no matter what that brings. Above all, make sure to talk to Steve. I know it's all my fault, but you know me, I just can't help myself. I craved the fun. I lived for the adventure."*

For a moment, Jenny swore to herself she could hear the trill of laughter, tinkling through the room, as if Cara were there. She gulped and looked down, knowing there was more...much more, but she couldn't bring herself to say the words, so she finished reading the letter silently. By the time she reached the end of it, she was sobbing.

She covered her face with her hands and felt an arm enfold her in a hug. She drew strength from the touch. "She was my best friend. The only one there when…" She couldn't tell him. If he knew just how broken she was, he wouldn't want her near him or Lola right now. She needed something to hold onto, just for a moment, to help her through the pain that squeezed her heart. A brief flash of intuition flared. If she felt like this, what must Steve feel?

"It's okay. God, I miss her too." Steve's voice was husky, and they held on tight. Jenny knew that in that instant, they drew support from each other.

"I brought her bag and things…like she asked me to." Her throat caught on the words as she forced them out.

Scrubbing at her face didn't stop the trails of tears from sliding down and soaking her skin. She drew in unsteady breaths and shoved up, out of the chair. Pacing the floor, she tried to clear the lump which had settled in her chest when Inspector Reid had told her Cara was dead.

"How did you… Where did the letter come from?" Steve asked.

She'd expected the question, so it was easy to answer. "The detective dealing with the case—Detective Inspector Reid—gave it to me. It's only a copy. The original was kept as evidence. They found it in her bra. She'd written it and then hid it. She'd obviously had time… They hadn't damaged her, I mean… Her body was unmarked except for the bullet wound, so they hadn't done anything." She stopped, swallowed the bile that rose in her throat, then gave herself a moment of composure, feeling him drag her into a hard embrace. "Initially they thought the letter might contain a clue to who her attacker was, but they quickly decided it didn't."

Steve grunted. She felt his nod and pushed out of his arms.

"I could…I could use another drink," she said.

He moved away, reached for his own glass, and gulped the rest of the amber liquid down.

Then he poured them both another generous amount. "You better sit down."

Jenny nodded and followed his instructions. Once cushioned on the chair, she sucked in a

deep breath. "I need to tell you how this happened. You need to decide if you want me to hang around and help solve this problem."

He gazed deeply into her eyes, as if examining whatever thought processes she had. "I don't think…"

"Steve, something in her background caused this to happen. I need to find out, and so do you. Inspector Reid indicated he thought it was no more than bad timing. But Cara was always careful. I explained that to him. She wouldn't stay in a dive, but that's where they found her. Why? Why was she there? Who was she meeting? Because it wasn't me. I didn't even know she was heading to Melbourne. None of this makes sense."

He handed her the glass and she drank deeply, the fire a little more muted than last time. He sloshed some more in her glass, and she glanced at him with question. But she was sure that tonight she'd need every bit of oblivion this drink could give her.

"Jenny, if this was more than a case of wrong place, wrong time, or wrong person—" She opened her mouth, but he raised a hand, cutting off her words.

"If there is more to this and she was targeted for some specific reason—and I honestly don't know if that's the case—then this is not something you want to be involved in. Hell, I'm not sure I should even be involved." He shook his head. "An investigation like this takes knowing people and a clear mind. Something I don't have at the moment." He sighed heavily. "I can ask questions, and like you, I need to know the truth, but Lola needs to be protected."

She slumped back in the chair, her mind whirling madly as she scrubbed her hand across her face. She came here simply to deliver Cara to her lover, but the more he questioned the circumstances, the more she felt driven to find out exactly what caused Cara's death.

"Tell me how you met her," Jenny said.

He jerked, her request obviously a surprise. "Why?"

Jenny's stomach turned cartwheels, and for a moment, the cloying thickness of grief and depression swirled. Not tonight, she promised herself, and closed her eyes, fighting off the sensation as best she could. She needed to know more.

"I met Cara the day she found Lola. Lola was a street kid, or so we originally thought. She'd been rummaging about in the trashcans and Cara couldn't leave her. She was so tiny. Not emaciated, but clearly hadn't eaten for days. Her hair was matted, and she had these big, scared eyes. I'll never forget that look. It felt so damned wrong that a kid would be so terrified. That was about five months ago."

Jenny opened her eyes, surprised they'd been together that long. Five long months and Cara hadn't said anything? That hurt more than anything else he'd said, because it indicated that Cara hadn't felt the level of affection toward her that she felt.

STEVE SAT ACROSS FROM JENNY, HIS LEGS SPLAYED AFTER THE highly emotional conversation, and

dragged his free hand through his hair. The glass dangled from one hand between his legs, and he gazed into the amber liquid.

Then he straightened, swished the drink, and lifted the glass, swallowing what was left, and sighed. "Cara called the police. My partner and I responded to the call. No one could work out who Lola was, and Child Services couldn't get out to see her for several days. They left her with Cara, and by then Lola had...well, not exactly bonded, but at least become comfortable with Cara. When they made contact with the government psychologist, it was recommended that Lola shouldn't be moved again. Not with her particular needs. It wasn't a perfect fit, but it worked." He looked up and he knew she saw the shadows in his eyes—hell, he'd seen them in the mirror himself. "The instant I met Cara and Lola, I thought they belonged together." Cara had left a hole in their lives no one could fill.

It was clear in her expression that Jenny felt the pull of Steve's grief. Her eyes held a sadness in the shadows that clouded her vision. Inexplicably, her understanding stung.

"I'm so sorry." Her words echoed the sorrow and grief that clawed at him.

Nothing could change what was. The woman he loved was dead. For a brief second, he wondered if anyone other than the three of them would attend the funeral and mourn her passing.

The thought sobered and scared him. Who would be there at the graveside to bid their farewells? It felt like a lonely, sad ending to a life lived briefly. He dragged his thoughts away.

Morbid introspection would only make matters worse. *** *

"Tell me what happened after Cara found Lola," Jenny said.

Steve rose, making his way toward her, and reached out a hand for her glass. He refilled it, handing it back to her before refilling his own. She was sure it was an avoidance tactic, dragging out the time before he'd have to tell her what had happened, no matter how hurtful.

She was willing to give him time, to let him compose himself and form an answer. This was what she did daily. It was a job she loved, but right now, right here, it felt overwhelming, and she wondered if this was how others felt, those who were traveling the path of grief. She reminded herself this wasn't about her, but helping Steve come to terms with his emotions.

Give the grieving time to work through their problems.

The clink of glass settling on the wooden benchtop was loud in the silence. When he turned back, a violent storm of anger brewed in his eyes. His hands shook a little, and the liquid in the glass sloshed against the sounds with an audible blop.

"That's when the threats started happening," he said. "Initially, it was just a message on her mobile phone or a letter. It quickly escalated though—bricks thrown at her car, animal entrails in the mailbox. She told me more than once that she was sure Lola knew who was stalking them, but we couldn't get her to talk. The government psychologist suggested we should leave her be for the moment, let her feel comfortable and settled. So we stopped asking. Lola's more relaxed now, but..." He shrugged, as if unable to quantify what it was that bothered him about this aspect of the situation.

Jenny agreed with the psychologist's advice. Forcing the child to talk would only make her sink more deeply into whatever ailed her.

He sat down heavily, and Jenny waited, sipping at the spirits in the glass again. Now that she'd become more used to the bite and fire of the alcohol, she could enjoy the subtle flavors of the rum.

"By the time Child Services came back, Lola was comfortable and Cara and I were in a..." Steve stopped, and a single tear tracked down his cheek. He humphed and cleared his throat, dashing at the moisture on his face. "We were in a relationship. So they were satisfied and left Lola with us. They arranged for Cara to consult further with a psychologist who diagnosed Lola's selective mutism. He believed it was caused by anxiety and some traumatic event. He felt she would benefit from his proposed agreement on living arrangements. Cara wasn't sure though."

Steve looked at her and she nodded.

"That was when Cara decided she needed to talk to you. I didn't want her to go even though things had settled. There'd been no further attacks, no more calls or visits, so she was sure everything was fine and safe. I guess something deep down told me that she was in danger, but Cara was emphatic. We argued, but she refused to change her mind, so I brought Lola here to stay with me until Cara returned. We'd been using Cara's place as our base." He shook his head. "That was a week ago. When I didn't hear from Cara, I knew something was wrong. I made enquiries, but she hadn't told me much about you, or how to contact you. I didn't even know where she was staying. Before she left she refused to tell me anything more than the basics of why she was going." His voice cracked.

Though she wanted to, Jenny didn't reach out to him. He'd bowed his head, clearly not wanting her intervention. So she watched, searching for signs he wanted her comfort. When he raised his head, his eyes were watery and red-rimmed. Jenny's heart ached for him.

"So I had to wait," he said.

Jenny put her hand to her stomach, trying to control the agony that bloomed, but it didn't abate. Cara had always been secretive. It was something that had driven Cara's mother nuts before she died.

Then a thought occurred to Jenny. "She never told you about me?"

He shook his head. "All I knew was you were some kind of psychologist, and you were in Melbourne. We didn't... Talking about our past wasn't something we spent a lot of time doing."

Jenny accepted that as the truth. Cara never liked revisiting the past, and she only told people what she wanted them to know. Her favorite saying was it's done, why bother about it again?

"So?" Steve spoke so quietly she had to bend closer to hear him.

"They found her in that hotel and contacted me through her phone records. There was no record of your number though. They checked to see who else they should contact. They couldn't break the encryption on her computer to access her address book."

Steve frowned. "But you could, and you emailed me. That was because of the letter, wasn't it?"

It was easy now to put the dots together, and she watched as he mentally connected all the links. "Yeah."

# CHAPTER THREE

Jenny was so easy to talk to. Steve poured out the story; her watchfulness told him she wasn't judging, just listening and letting him grieve. The pressure that had built in his chest, the suffocating ball of anger and regret, melted away with every word he spoke.

The only time Jenny interrupted was to clarify a point or to ask for more information, as if she knew exactly how to extract the final knot of pain.

Cara hadn't been a listener. She'd talked and prattled, sharing news and gossip with abandon. Right now, he needed this woman's ear. It was a balm to his soul. He needed a calm voice, and the soft, soothing touches that reminded him of his mother. She offered that and comfort that none of his male friends could extend.

Then he damned himself for the unfair mental comparison. After all, Jenny was a psychologist, and Cara had said she was very good at what she did. And he'd loved Cara, hadn't he? So how could he do that to her memory?

He squinted into his drink, lifted it, and swallowed it down. Jenny did the same then put the glass down carefully on the table and rose, wobbling a little. He reached out to help her, noting how the room seemed to shimmer beneath his feet.

"Sorry, not shure why the room is shpinning," he said.

He saw the small smile on her face and how something in her eyes lightened. It opened a chink inside his chest, and he smiled at her.

"It could be we've had a few drinks. And qwitch...quite quickly." He held out a hand. "Come on, it's time for ush cho go cho bed." He blinked, knowing how slurred his words sounded even to his own ears.

Jenny giggled a little, her gaze less than clear. She covered her mouth with her hand, her eyes blinking owlishly.

He noticed how fine her skin was, and when Jenny shivered he pulled her close. "You cold?" He looked at her and frowned. "I think I'f had a few choo many."

She nodded and smiled. "I think we've both misjudged how much we've drunk." She hiccupped and blushed. Her lashes fluttered a little against her skin and he watched, mesmerized, only to pull away again. "D'you...do you need to check Lola?" She swayed slightly in front of him, and he nodded, then regretted the action. "Che's... She's on the way."

Jenny started to make her way toward the hall, then stilled before he could reach her. "You know, I don't... I rarely drink anything. It's not..." Her blush was deeper again, and he couldn't help the momentary flash of protectiveness.

Steve gave a half-nod, unwilling to examine what drove the emotions rising in him. "Me either. This isn't..."

"It's stress. I should have known better."

"Which means we need... Time for bed." He held out a hand, then his fingers gripped hers, linking around them, and they moved up the corridor, their hips bumping and sliding together.

His body felt scorched by her nearness, and when he reached Lola's room and peered within, he stepped away.

Jenny whispered, "She's sleeping soundly."

"She is." The relief cleared his head just slightly.

Once assured that Lola was safe for the night, he walked with Jenny to the bedroom at the

end of the hall. Confusion filled him once more as they moved on. When they arrived at her door, she placed her hand on the knob, but her fingers slipped. He placed one of his hands over hers.

They had to work together to open it, and she giggled as it flew open. They jostled together and used each other to balance precariously in the entry.

"Well..." The husky tone of her voice echoed through his body.

"Well."

She turned, her eyes seeking his, and in the depths he saw a flash of hunger and loneliness. "I should...I should go to bed."

He blinked at her words and watched as she tottered to the bed. He told himself it was

only concern that she didn't fall over that made him followed her in, and he caught her as she fell to the satin cover. She tugged him or he tugged her, it didn't matter once they were on the mattress together.

"Jenny..." His lips caught her cheek and she turned toward him, her lips parting. He saw the startled surprise in the depths of her eyes and the way they fluttered closed as skin touched

She tasted amazing. Soft and succulent. He leaned closer, letting his body slide against hers. Felt her feminine figure mold against his and knew the minute she felt his arousal. Hunger flared, a wild conflagration that started with a moan.

Her hands slipped up around his neck, every nerve singing with joyous abandonment as the kiss deepened. His tongue found hers, and she made a mewling sound in the back of her throat.

It galvanized him into action, thoughts scattering wildly as a rush of desire crested. He pushed her back against the pillows, and his hand roamed, searching for the mound of her breast hidden beneath the ugly, black blouse.

She shuddered and arched into his touch, while his free hand quested, looking for her waistband, and burrowed beneath it. Hot, satiny skin quivered under his touch.

She let go of him, and her hands, wobbly and unsure, worked at his shirt, popping the buttons. He raised his head and looked at her. Jenny's face glowed in the dim light, her eyes shining, and for an instant, the merest hint of reality flashed within him. He almost pulled away, but then she moved, causing him to slide against her. With a growl, he dipped his head as she rose up, her chest heaving. The tip of her luscious pink tongue peeked out from between her plump lips and mesmerized him. The last of his mental defenses melted away, and he gave in to the craving that hollowed his belly.

Jenny pushed the shirt from his shoulders and placed her lips to his chest. He shuddered under the onslaught as a myriad of sensual needs exploded within him.

His skin and chest burned under her homage, and any vestige of his usual skill fled. Her tongue flicked at his skin, laving his nipples, and he hissed as he tugged at her blouse, needing more. Jenny pulled back, letting him strip it away, and he saw her black bra beneath. It barely contained her lush curves, and he salivated, knowing they were for him. Her nipples jutted proud against the lycra, and he slid his thumb slowly over a nub. She quaked and cried out, her eyes closing as she strained. The tip grew and she gyrated her hips against his, lost in the same web as he.

Her clever fingers found his erection, dancing for an instant over the straining zipper, and then the button was undone and the zipper rasping as she pulled the cloth from his body.

She moaned again, and his heart raced with excitement. One hand worked behind her back, struggling with the clasp of her bra, while the other sought and found the closure of her pants. Once he had them undone he murmured brokenly, "Lift your hips."

She raised her bottom, and the cotton hiding the glorious length of her legs came away as his body burned. Now that her bra clasp had released, her breast slid free, and he moaned, seeing one generous nipple poking out. His breath left in a whoosh as his groin tightened at the sight of the raspberry tip.

"Oh, Jenny. You're so beautiful and hot."

"Steve?"

Her voice called like a siren, and he shucked the rest of his clothes as she fumbled with her panties, then he was on her, covering her body with his. The feel of her against him nearly had him coming as his cock glided against the skin of her belly.

His skin burned everywhere it touched hers. He skimmed his hand down her body, sliding his fingers between the curls he discovered, before dipping between the cleft. His fingers found her core and the tiny nub. He pressed down and she bucked against him, and he slid two fingers deeply inside, the dampness easing his way. Her legs moved as he sought the secrets of her body, but it wasn't enough. He needed to be buried within her.

Her legs shifted further, and he withdrew his fingers, which were coated with moisture. Her eyes opened as he licked his tongue over the wetness between her legs. "Sweet and wet. And so damned hot."

Now he moved deliberately, his hands sliding over the flesh of her thighs as he positioned himself at the juncture of her beautiful, white legs. His cock nudged at her entry, and he paused, giving her one last chance to stop the intimacy, but she merely wound her legs around him and squeezed. With that, he thrust deep and hard. The rasp of intimate body parts joining urged him on to fill her.

She cried out, arched up, and he moved again. She squirmed against him, her fingers digging into his shoulders as the wild dance took over. Again and again he thrust, felt her meet him halfway until she cried out, holding herself taut, and he shoved home one last time. The glorious milking sensation of her sheath drove him to a climax such as he'd never known before. He was sure he would pass out from the exquisite sensations that consumed him. It continued on and on as his release overcame himself while hilt deep within her body.

"Oh God!" he cried and slumped forward, his heart beating a

fierce tattoo. He closed his eyes and sleep caught him up, rocked him gently in its arms as the world melted away.

SOMETHING WOKE HER. JENNY WASN'T QUITE SURE WHAT IT was, but her body ached almost as much as her head did, particularly her breasts, and there was a delicious throb between her thighs.

"Ugh." Her mouth was dry and sandpapery, and her face felt scraped raw.

She turned and heard an oomph close to her face. She cracked open an eyelid and nearly shrieked seeing a dark head on the pillow. A broad chest lay next to her on the bed, and her gaze followed the line of hair down the length of the male body barely hidden beneath the white sheet.

"Oh. My. God." She breathed the words as silently as she could, backing away.

He stirred with a grunt, rolling toward her, one large arm landing on her naked stomach. *Naked! I'm naked! How in heaven's name did that happen?* Disjointed memories—at least she thought they were memories—flooded her mind, and she shied away. *This was Cara's man. Not hers. How could she?*

She wanted to cry but contained herself as she tugged at the weight locking her still.

"Stay still, Cara." He muttered the words into the pillow, and she felt lower than a snake's belly.

*What have I done?* The answer, though, was clear. She'd had sex with her newly-dead best friend's lover!

She couldn't even blame the alcohol, because she'd been attracted to him before taking a drink. No. She was lower than any kind of reptile. Self-recrimination rained down upon her, and she sat lost in the whirl of misery as his eyes opened.

"Jesus Christ! What are you doing here? Naked?" He reared back and seemed to note he was in her bedroom as his bloodshot eyes took in the decor. "Oh Christ!" The loathing in his voice flayed at her. He pulled away quickly, his eyes filled with horror and disgust.

For just a second she wondered...if she had been as thin as Cara, would he have pulled away quite so quickly? She looked down at her bare, pendulous breasts then back at him. The look in his eyes echoed the curl of derision on his lips.

She raised shaking hands to cover herself as she scooted over the linen. His eyes closed, and she took the opportunity to clamber over the edge and head for the bathroom, swiftly locking the door behind her before dropping to the floor. A sob wracked her body as she remembered the distaste on his face.

A knock on the bathroom door had her raising her head. "What?" The word shot from her lips as her soul shriveled to nothing.

"I'm sorry..." His voice died away and silence descended.

Her brain screamed out me too, but her heart stopped the words from finding a voice. She stayed there, feeling the cool tiles beneath her burning hot skin. She'd never been perfect—all she had to do was look in the mirror to know that—yet she had never before sunk so low.

Jenny refused to blame the alcohol. No, she'd made the decision in her mind, subconscious or not, and it was she who had to pay the price. She looked around, found a towel, and covered her nude body.

Gathering as much dignity as she could muster, she opened the door. "If you'll give me a few minutes, I'll call a taxi and be out of your hair."

He frowned. "You don't need to leave."

She shook her head, her hair whipping to and fro. "No, I really should."

His lips firmed. "I really don't think that would be a good idea."

She opened her mouth to argue, but he raised a hand.

"Trust me on this." He held up his phone, the one he must have dug out of the pants he

now wore...without a shirt. He showed her a photo of the three of them at the airport. The text message was brutal apparently, because his gaze turned flat and she couldn't read more than anger in their depths. "You've been seen and tagged."

She snapped her mouth shut, understanding what he just told her. Their conversation from last night was fuzzy, but she recollected the majority of it.

"Oh God…"

"Yeah, so get dressed. I'll make us both a coffee." He leaned toward her, as if clearing away her distress was the most important thing on his mind. "You do drink coffee, don't you?"

Jenny nodded slowly, realizing he was hoping to calm the recriminations that whirled around inside her head. If only it were so easy to overcome what she'd done. What they'd both done.

"Then I'll see you in the kitchen in a few minutes." He left the room, holding his shirt in his hands.

STEVE SHOOK WITH ANGER AND SELF-LOATHING AS HE wandered into the kitchen. A glance at the clock told him it was early, barely five o'clock, and he checked on Lola as his memories surged.

The child was still asleep, lying soft and innocent in her bed. His gut churned. He'd just had sex with Jenny, Cara's best friend, down the hall from the sleeping girl. What's more, if the state of his head was anything to go by, he also had a serious headache to contend with. Cara hadn't even been buried yet and he was tomcatting on her. He shook his head, heartily sickened by his behavior.

How in hell had that happened? But he knew the ugly truth. The alcohol, loneliness, and a warm body had been irresistible in his weakened emotional state. He barked a laugh at the thought. Yeah, his weakened emotional state was a cop-out. He'd chosen to have sex, no matter how inebriated he was.

He banged around in the kitchen, readying cups and coffee. Each move jarred his fragile head, but he wasn't complaining. He deserved a whole heap more ass-kicking before he could chalk this up to experience.

The smell of brewing coffee filled the air, and he grabbed sugar and milk, slammed them to the counter, then reached for a teaspoon. "How could you do that?" He wanted to snarl aloud but kept his recriminations to quiet, anguished murmurs instead. It wouldn't do to wake Lola until he and Jenny had talked this through.

Memories of Jenny's body beneath his exploded through him. Soft skin and warm touches... He forced the memory back. In its place came her look of horror and shock, and then the brittle dignity she'd clad herself in when she'd offered to leave.

She'd clearly accepted full responsibility, and expected to be sent out into the world to fend for herself. That stung his manly pride too.

He was one half of the situation, and he'd take his lumps like a man.

Jenny entered the kitchen, her face pale. He read pure anguish in her eyes at their actions. Her pupils had dilated, and the whites of her eyes were pink from crying. It pulled him up hard, and he sighed.

"Dammit..."

"No, Steve. It's my fault. I really should leave." Her voice was so quiet he had to strain to hear it. Her bottom lip quivered, and he felt even worse than before. "I don't think I should go to the funeral."

The words stopped him dead. The funeral. Today he would finalize all the plans and tomorrow...they'd be burying Cara. He had to face the truth that less than two days before he buried the woman he'd loved, he'd sunk himself hilt deep into her best friend. What kind of person did that make him? Self-loathing rode hard on him and nausea rose, but he breathed through it. *I'm an animal, not a man.* No gentleman would do something as vile as this. For the first time he was pleased his parents didn't live to see what he'd become.

He shook his head, pouring the hot water over the instant coffee in the cups. "You can't leave. They've already worked out you're involved somehow in this whole mess. They got a photo of us at the airport, and they messaged it to me, which means they know my number." He looked up and saw the hurt and bewildered look in her eyes. It stopped him in his tracks.

"But...don't you know who it was that sent it? Can't you trace it somehow?"

He shook his head. "No. I tried, but it's a blocked number."

"I... It feels wrong though, for me to be here. After..." She moistened her lips, and his heart ached.

"I know what you mean."

Jenny shook her head. "No, you don't...you can't."

A frisson of apprehension filled him. A recollection of Cara sitting at this very bench just days before she'd left, talking about her friend who happened to be a psychologist. It was the first he'd heard of Jenny's existence.

"My friend's a psychologist. Really good at what she does. She's had it rough and still struggles with her own issues. She understands what her patients are dealing with, and that makes her fantastic at her job, but she's brittle and easily broken. I worry about her."

Realization bloomed; now he understood what Cara had told him about how broken Jenny was.

Jenny looked at him. "Trust me, it's better for everyone if I leave."

He heard the desperation in her words. "How could it be better for everyone? If they find you, they'll kill you...just like they did Cara." His voice was harsh as he bent toward her. "Look, we both did something stupid. It's not as if either of us is incapable of dealing with reality."

She reared back, and he wondered what on earth he'd said now.

"Yeah, well, while you're making those assumptions, tell me how I got these then?" her waspish voice demanded as she thrust both wrists forward. He saw the white lines crisscrossing her wrists.

His stomach soured. Then he remembered his words. Jesus, this just went from bad to worse. Slash marks faded to white, but never left. Telltale scars that told of deep pain that left people thinking there could be no future.

"Oh God. Jenny... I don't know what to say."

She shoved away from the bench, and he reached out to grab her.

"Let me go!" She twisted in his arms, fighting to free herself, but something deep inside told him to keep her close.

"No." He sucked down a gulp of air, her fragrance filling his head. "You're staying. I

can't and won't let you go out there. It's too dangerous."

She stilled in his arms. "Look, I get that you were a policeman. I understand your need to protect. But who will protect you from me? And..." She shuddered and shook her head as if unwilling to say anything further.

He closed his eyes for a second, knowing that his actions had brought her down to this level of emotional turmoil. He'd heard the defeat in her tone and a chink in his heart opened. "Don't go...not yet. Help me find out what's wrong with Lola and what happened to

Cara." He whispered the words into her fragrant hair.

She stood for a long moment. Perhaps she was considering her options? Her shoulders slumped. His stomach jittered at the knowledge that he'd caused her further pain. "It may not be that simple."

The husky tone of her voice told him she was still overcome by her emotions, but some of the tension released from his muscles.

"I know, but I think Lola knows the secret." The words slipped out.

Jenny pulled away. "I'll stay a few days longer. For Lola, because that's what Cara would want me to do." She blinked. "Give me a minute to grab my laptop, and then you can tell me what you know."

She turned and left him standing in the kitchen looking at the blank wall.

# CHAPTER FOUR

Jenny watched as the trees whipped by. Sitting beside Steve in the car was torturous. They were close enough to touch, but the air surrounding them chilled her to the bone. What was yet to come would no doubt stretch her to her limits.

At the funeral home, she wrapped her arms around herself as the undertaker accepted the bag of clothing she'd brought. He was around sixty, with gray hair and faded blue eyes. The lines on his face reminded her he'd seen it all before. His demeanor was restful, and she was thankful Cara would be attended to by a caring man like him.

"It was her favorite dress. I thought..." Jenny said, her words trailing off.

"That's fine, Miss Douglas. We'll make sure she looks peaceful and happy. Our handlers are highly skilled at their jobs." He turned in Steve's direction. "There are just a few things we need to deal with." The man's voice was soothing, but the pain that wrought its way through Jenny grew and bloomed.

They took a seat at the desk, and the undertaker stashed the bag of clothing on the table behind him.

"You stated you didn't want a viewing, or at least a public one, Mr. Davies. Is that correct?"

"I... No. I'd like the opportunity to say goodbye, but..."

It was clear Steve was struggling and—even though she still felt unfaithful—she stretched out her hand, gripped his, and exhaled relief when he squeezed it. She wouldn't look. He needed his dignity intact, and after last night... She gulped, the guilt burying her once more.

"Of course, since she has no immediate family, it makes sense to have a private viewing. We can arrange that for later today or first thing tomorrow morning...whatever suits your needs."

He choked beside Jenny, and that squeezed her heart even harder. She turned and the tears gathering in his eyes as he implored her to answer gave her the strength she needed. She looked at the undertaker. "We need to discuss when would be best, as there is Lola to consider too. Can we...can we get back to you later today?"

The man nodded. "Of course. Now, as to the actual ceremony, you've indicated she was a non-believer?"

Jenny was on solid ground here, because they'd discussed this several times as they grew up together. Cara had many times raised her disdain for anything religious, to the point that Jenny had stopped attending organized youth associations in her early teens, rather than lose Cara as her friend.

"Yes," Jenny replied. "She believed there was nothing afterward, so any ceremony should be non-religious."

Steve shifted beside her as if surprised by her assertion. "That's not...that's not what she told me."

Jenny frowned and glanced quickly toward him. "She used to tell me that believing in an after-life was nonsense." She bit her lip. What if Cara's beliefs had changed sometime after Jenny had left for Melbourne? "Of course she could have changed her mind."

"I don't know. I mean, she came to church with me once or twice, but now that you say that, she didn't seem comfortable or to know much about…" His face shuttered. "I think it would be best to go with the non-denominational option."

It felt strange that Steve didn't know what Cara believed in, but she tucked that away for consideration later. Right now, they needed to focus on giving Cara the send-off she deserved.

"That's fine. We need a list of maybe two or three songs that were important to her, of most importance are the ones for the entry of the casket and the internment, since there will only be the graveside ceremony." The undertaker steepled his fingers. "Is there any way of guessing the number of attendees?"

Steve shook his head and shrugged, clearly at a loss, so Jenny cleared her throat. "She has no family, and there was really only her and me in the last few years. It would just be how many from Steve's friends."

She waited for him to speak. "A dozen perhaps, maybe two," he said.

"So we'll work on a small and intimate number then." The undertaker nodded his understanding.

At that, a sob escaped Jenny. It was real. All of it. The bubble of pain inside her grew again, expanding so that it squashed her lungs. She tried to subdue the wracking sound, needed to stifle it, but another aching wail emerged. Biting her knuckle didn't stop it, and this time it was Steve who was there. He sheltered her in his arms and held her close as she dealt with the awful reality that Cara, her best friend, was gone.

In the car on the way home, Steve examined the meeting in his mind. They'd both been through an emotional wringer, and tears had threatened at times, but it was Jenny who'd tried so hard to be strong that she had finally caved in when they started dealing with the details of the service.

Cara had never let on that she didn't believe in a hereafter. He'd taken that for granted. It felt like maybe he didn't know her as well as he'd thought he did, but dammit...they'd been so close! He'd never felt for any other woman the way he had about her.

Then again, he'd never felt for another woman the way he did for Jenny. His stomach dipped.

She was silent, curled into herself in the seat beside him with her eyes closed. At the traffic lights, he allowed himself a moment of quiet contemplation. She was different—an enigma. It was clear she'd had a hard life. That showed in the scars on her wrists and the guarded way she interacted with others. In fact, the only person she didn't hold up a barrier to was Lola.

Lola. She hadn't spoken a word since he'd known her, but he felt sure that she knew something important, and whatever it was, it was likely the key to her mutism. "Look, about Lola. Do you think there's anything..."

Jenny opened her eyes and gazed in his direction. "It really depends on the underlying reasons behind her mutism. She has to be ready to talk and have someone she feels comfortable with before anything there can be resolved."

"But she seems...I don't know...comfortable with you."

She barked out a laugh. "It's my job. I deal with pediatric patients and those with extreme reactions on a daily basis."

The words left him feeling hollow. Did she really believe that? "No. You've got this touch. It's soothing and..." When she sighed he frowned. "You disagree?"

"I'm as confused as anyone else, Steve. I'm not a miracle worker, nor do I have all the answers, so don't expect me to magically whip up something that will cure Lola's mutism. It's never that simple."

Her self-deprecation ate at him. For the first time in his life, he felt at sea with a woman. When his stomach rumbled, he took it as a sign not to examine the situation any further. "Okay then, let's change the subject and grab some lunch."

That caught her attention and she turned back in his direction. "Lunch?"

He couldn't suppress a laugh. "Yes. It's something you do in the middle of the day when you're hungry."

"But I look like...I'm a mess." Jenny dragged her fingers through the long, black hair he

knew from experience felt like silk.

"There's nothing wrong with the way you look. Besides, it's been an emotional morning.

It's okay to not look our best." Heaven knew his own eyes were pink, but as much as he ached with Cara's loss, his stomach continued to rumble. "There's this little pizzeria down by the pier. It's never busy at this time of day, and Gino...he knew Cara too. It seems like the right place to go."

Jenny shrugged, her eyes signaling she was more than a little disbelieving that Cara had visited a pizza place. Clearly, the Cara she'd known was all about the diet and the looks, and that confused him. After all, a person could change, right?

"Sure. Since it was yours and Cara's place, it seems right."

Instead of accepting his assertion, though, her brow remained deeply furrowed, highlighting the dark bruises beneath her eyes while she radiated her 'I'm not sure about what you've told me' attitude.

With a deep, heaving sigh, Steve clicked on the car's indicator.

When they arrived home, Steve thanked the babysitter. The woman assured him she was happy to help, and after bidding a quick goodbye to Lola, she was on her way.

Lola gifted Jenny with a shy smile, and Jenny smiled back. Jenny realized the need to be careful and not crowd the young girl. Could she possibly find the underlying cause of Lola's issues in a few days? She itched to grab her psychology texts, but they were in Melbourne. All she had was her computer, and the cursory research she'd done offered no help or solutions. She would need to delve deeper to find out what caused the child to withdraw totally.

"Hey, Lola, would you like to show me your room?" As an opening went, it wasn't the best, but right now she needed to form some kind of connection with the little girl.

Lola focused on Jenny, her brown eyes assessing the woman in front of her as if weighing up whether she was friend or foe. The guarded response reinforced for Jenny that some trauma had made the girl wary and untrusting of adults. It was the direct opposite to how most five and six year olds would react. During training, they'd had to work with socially adjusted children in an effort to work out what was considered within the norms of behavior. She'd noted that they tended to be sunny, welcoming, and likely gregarious, all of which were the opposite of the child in front of her.

When Lola held out her hand, Jenny smiled, feeling as if she'd passed some important test.

On the way to the bedroom, she noted the fine tremors in Lola's grasp. But the grip was tight, as if she were desperate for someone to trust. Then and there, Jenny made a silent vow to do anything she could to protect the child from any further harm. Lola settled down on the bed and rubbed her eyes.

On the fluffy, pink bed sat a stuffed dog. Jenny smiled. "When I was a little girl, I had a stuffed dog too. His name was Alfie. I wonder if your dog has a name."

The girl shook her head and hugged it close to her side.

"He made me feel safe. I'd sleep with him on my pillow, and I'm sure he told me more than once I was his best friend." Jenny continued to chatter to the little girl.

Lola smiled faintly, and Jenny grinned. "Can I sit down?"

Lola nodded and patted the bed to indicate Jenny could sit next to her.

She moved carefully, ensuring nothing she did would scare the child. "Do you have a favorite book? Mine was about a bunny that had lots of children and wanted to be the Easter Bunny."

She waited as Lola scampered off the bed, tugged a book from the small bookshelf by the closet, and brought it over.

She smiled seeing the title of the book. "I like that book too. Caterpillars are lots of fun. Have you ever made a caterpillar out of cupcakes?"

The little girl's eyes grew round, and she shook her head.

"Well, depending on how long I'm here, maybe we should do that? It would be fun." Lola grinned, and Jenny's heart lurched ever so slightly as twin dimples appeared on the little girl's cheeks. If only she were more normal.

A flash of memory, in all its unwelcome glory, flicked through her brain, and Jenny shook her head, chasing it away.

Lola was watching her steadily.

Jenny hunched down to the child's level. "When I was your age, I had to share my room with my little brother. Yuck!"

Lola grinned for a second before the emotion disappeared.

"Well, Miss Lola. Thank you for showing me your room. It's lovely. Would you like a drink?"

The little girl nodded and shyly held out her hand. The simple act, artless and without the weighing up she'd done before, spoke volumes to Jenny. Together they meandered down to the kitchen, but still Jenny couldn't help wondering about Lola.

She must have a family, parents who were worried sick about her. Lola was far too young to be so alone. That made Lola even more special to her.

## CHAPTER FIVE

Jenny watched as they lowered Cara's casket into the grave. Her chest ached, and her eyes screamed with pain. God, it seemed so very wrong to be standing there watching the scene unfold before her. She'd wept during the brief graveside service, paroxysms of grief tearing at her, and felt Steve sitting upright beside her the whole time. Cold and aloof, stiff and hollow as the celebrant said the final words before the pallbearers, arranged by the funeral home, stood and hefted the wooden box containing Cara's remains from the stand and onto their shoulders. The walk to the open maw of her grave was mere feet, but the action seemed to take forever. Then they placed the casket on the straps, waiting.

*I should leave. I don't belong here with them.* Lola had grabbed her hand, and she was grateful the child needed her support. That someone needed her gave her a modicum of comfort right now. It helped her control the anguish that battled deep inside her.

Roiling emotions battered and buffeted her as surely as a rock in the middle of the wild ocean. She was scared she'd cave in, give in to depression again, so she bit her lip and worked at beating down the wild storm brewing.

The flight reflex urged her to leave while she was still able to. But she couldn't. She'd given her word, and it was the very last thing Cara had asked of her.

Cara had stayed by her side when she most needed a friend, during her psychiatric treatments. Cara had been the one who'd rung the ambulance after finding her on the floor of the bathroom that fateful day while ribbons of scarlet blood had decorated the tiles. She had remained in the hospital as Jenny lay sedated and alone.

Now her best friend lay cold and lifeless in that box. Jenny watched as the pallbearers took up the long, white straps and lowered the casket into the ground. The rubbing sound of the webbing slipping through gloved hands grated loudly to her super-sensitive hearing. She barely noticed the beating of the hot sun, only the misery that clouded her mind.

Cara's death was wrong on so many fronts, and Jenny felt the injustice of it keenly.

The undertaker reached for a clod of dirt and threw it onto the box. It hit with a thud. "From the earth we rose, and to the earth we'll return." His voice was quiet.

Steve stepped forward. He urged the child to do the same, and Jenny heard the twin sounds of earth hitting wood. It was real. It was now. It was time to say goodbye.

Her chest wound tighter than it had ever been before as she stepped forward and leaned

down. Felt the dirt in her fingers, catching under her fingernails while tears tracked down her face. The finality of the act nearly overwhelmed her, and she let the dirt dribble through the fingers she held over the gaping hole.

"Goodbye, Cara," she whispered as her vision clouded.

Then she turned and walked away. It was the hardest thing she'd done in her life. She stumbled along until a hand gripped her shoulder.

"Come on." Steve's tight voice echoed in her mind.

The pain and anguish inside her was so real she wanted to cry out at the injustice of it. It should have been her in the box. Then Cara, Steve, and Lola could be a family. It was wrong— she felt that to the marrow of her bones—but she couldn't turn back time. She couldn't give away the pain that ripped through her or Steve, or even little Lola, who burrowed into the skirts of Jenny's ugly, black dress.

Unable to go any further, she stopped and opened her mouth to protest. Steve's arms wound around her. Jenny sank into them, needing the comfort and desperate to return what she could.

She didn't care if anyone saw them or there were any repercussions. Steve and Lola needed support too, and she wouldn't let either of them down. She'd already made one mistake, and she'd be damned if she'd make another.

They stood like that for endless moments. Alone and lost in their private grief. She registered dimly that people walked by, some touching Steve on the shoulder, showing their understanding of his pain. Others gave them a wide berth, probably not knowing what to say.

She raised her head, stepped away, and scrubbed at her face. Clearing her throat was difficult because it ached viciously, as did her brain. "We should head to the wake."

He nodded and gazed at her. She felt the loss of his warmth. Lola though stayed plastered to her side, and she kept her arm around the shivering child. They walked away from the quiet enclosure, past monuments to those lost, leaving Cara in her cold bed. Jenny didn't look back...couldn't look back, because she knew if she did the pain would overtake her. Right now she needed her equilibrium to get through the rest of today. One day at a time was all she could ask for.

Steve took Jenny's hand, wrapped it around his arm, and led her to his car, waiting beyond the gates of the cemetery.

"I should go home."

He glanced in her direction, his gaze narrowing. "What?" The chill in his voice cut through her.

"Well, you and Lola should have time alone—"

"Don't, Jenny. You need closure as much as we do. Please, I

would—" He swallowed. "Look, even if you don't come for you, come for Lola. Please?"

He needed her there, she realized. In that instant she knew, no matter how much she ached, she'd stay.

They climbed into the car, and as Steve pulled away a cold, prickling sensation seeped through Jenny's bones. "Steve..." She touched his hand.

He nodded. "I know. We need to get out of here."

Even as he spoke a large black van loomed. Steve drove the car forward, the engine whining through gear changes, wheels spinning in the dirt before gaining traction on the asphalt. The van veered across to cut off their exit.

Jenny moved instinctively, throwing her arm out across the gap between the seats. Lola cried out from the back seat. The van came so close she could almost see within it, and again it veered. This time metal screamed as it scraped against the vehicle, and the car fishtailed. Jenny lurched against the restraint of her seatbelt. Steve swore loudly while the car jerked then shot out of the parking area. Car horns blared as they punched their way onto the road.

"Steve?" A quick glance in the mirror showed the black van halted on the side of the road. Adrenalin pulsed wildly through Jenny as she turned to Lola, fearing the child was hurt, but though Lola had hooked her fingers through the seatbelts and clutched them in tiny, white- knuckled hands, and her eyes were wide with fright, she seemed intact. "Are you okay, Lola?"

The child nodded, and Jenny closed her eyes, giving a tiny prayer of thanks that someone was looking out for them.

STEVE SWORE AS THE CAR SLEWED INTO THE TRAFFIC. HE HELD the wheel and said a silent prayer for help. He heard Jenny's shriek, but couldn't react to it. Not yet. Dimly, he knew that Jenny had been ready to save the child. He thanked heaven for her and her quick reaction.

"We can't stop here," he said. "We need to get somewhere safe."

Jenny stared at him, her face white with terror. "What do you plan to do?"

"It's time to call in a favor." He punched a button on the console, and the sound of dialing filled the air. Relief filled him when the call was answered promptly. At least something was going to plan.

"Dave here."

"It's Steve. They came at us as we left the cemetery." His gaze scanned the rearview mirror, looking for a sign they were being followed. He couldn't see anything, but his stomach roiled at the thought of the close shave. The woman in the seat next to him sat ramrod straight, her lips pulled thin.

"Shit! Are you okay?"

"Yeah." He let loose a short, mirthless laugh. His training had saved them again. He wondered idly if his past could be blamed for all that had gone wrong in his life too.

"Where are you?"

He heard a rustle. Dave was no doubt fishing around in his pocket for a notepad and pen. "Heading north on the motorway. We'll go to the wake, make an appearance, and leave.

Can you arrange an escort to meet us there? We'll head directly home after."

He felt rather than saw Jenny's nod, and the bands around his chest loosened a bit. She understood, and that made him feel a little more comfortable. She hadn't fallen apart in the face of what was—no doubt for her—a scary and unfamiliar experience. It was another big plus for the woman.

"We'll be waiting outside," Dave replied.

Steve slowed the car and indicated to enter the grounds of the small cafe where he'd organized a reception in celebration of Cara's life. Dave stood outside, along with some of his other police buddies. He pulled the car into the nearest empty spot and stopped the engine. He sat still for a moment, letting the adrenaline wash from his system. Now he simply felt drained and exhausted.

His eyes closed, but like an old reel-to-reel, the entire incident replayed in his mind. His gut churned, and his head felt like it might explode.

"You did well." Jenny's quiet words soothed the raging anger that filled him.

He could have died...Lola too. Or Jenny. Sharp fingers of pain gripped at his heart, squeezing even tighter than before.

"I got us out in one piece, but they mean business. We have to treat this seriously." He opened his eyes, pinning her with his gaze. She smiled. It was wobbly but beautiful. The trust in her eyes warmed him through.

"You're right, but we did survive. You did what you had to, and because of that, all three of us are sitting here alive." She looked over his shoulder. Clearly something had caught her attention. "Your friends are heading this way."

He heard the click and rasp of her seatbelt, then she opened the door and headed to Lola's door.

The little girl all but leapt into Jenny's arms. Lola burrowed into the embrace, eyes squeezed tightly shut, and he had a vision of the three of them, hand in hand, walking down a beach when this was over. He thrust the thought away. It didn't belong there. Not now, and certainly not today. Today was for Cara and the memories he cherished. His breathing turned ragged. He hadn't seen those daydreams with Cara, and surely to God he shouldn't see them with Jenny. He'd loved Cara. Hadn't he?

The thought pierced him. Had he really loved Cara or the life she had represented? He shied away from the thought. It was wrong to think like this on the day he had buried her. But it remained, a seed of doubt at the back of his mind, gnawing away at him.

His friends gathered around the car while Dave inspected the damage. He fought to contain his frustration. His mind whirled madly at the questions, and he looked over Dave's head, seeing how Jenny protectively cradled Lola in her arms.

He answered the questions the men fired at him as honestly as he could. Dave clapped his shoulder. "Mate, we're looking into the situation with Lola and the threats. But with Cara gone... well, we don't have a lot of leads."

He knew what that meant. They weren't even supposed to be investigating it since the murder took place interstate. "I could—"

"Don't go getting involved, Steve. You're not official anymore."

He pulled away, wanting to yell that the answer was there, staring them in the face. All he needed was a hint. They just weren't looking in the right place, he knew it deep down. They were doing everything they could, but were bound by conventions and rules. He no longer was though. He had connections and money.

"Dave, just leave it for the moment. I can't deal with this right now." He shook his head. He needed them to think it was grief talking and making him act strangely, otherwise they'd question him further, wonder at what he was doing and maybe connect his behavior to the past. He couldn't afford for them to work out that he had no intention of letting this go. He stepped away from the vehicle.

His friend shot him a look of disbelief. They'd known each other too long for Dave to believe he'd just drop it, but this wasn't the time or place to discuss it.

Steve gazed at Jenny. "Let's go inside."

Jenny nodded, as did his friends, and they trooped inside. People sat in small groups of threes and fours while the buzz of hushed conversations filled the air. He wandered between the chairs as people stood and hugged him, laid soft hands on his arm and shoulder.

Jenny had veered off to the other side of the room, found an empty seat, and sat down with Lola in her lap. He saw the way her fingers gently pushed the strands of hair away from Lola's face and his mind stopped. Her caring attitude toward Lola had turned his mind to mush.

Over the months he and Cara had been looking after the little girl, he'd started to think of her as his. His daughter. His child. She might not be biologically his, but the bond had been forged. Deep and rich. Powerful.

He'd lost his quicksilver fairy, Cara. He couldn't lose Lola too. He'd do whatever it took to keep her. A plan formulated in his mind. It made his belly churn. It was calculated, and he'd get the benefits along with Lola. He shied away from the thought that Jenny would be the loser in the equation.

His parents had left him what others might call a fortune, so he was more than comfortable financially. He could afford not to work and keep Lola happy and well cared for. At least until she had settled into a routine and started school. Or until he found a wife.

Steve made a mental note to discuss the situation with Jenny. Watching the way she interacted with Lola, he was sure that she would agree.

He smiled. It was perfect. He ignored the voice in the back of his head that called him a liar. The one that whispered that he was using the opportunity to keep Jenny around. Steve felt quite satisfied.

# CHAPTER SIX

The trip home from the wake was silent. They arrived early enough that the sun still shone in the sky, and Lola retreated to the backyard, like any normal five or six year old, the swing set squeaking in the quiet housing estate. The surreal atmosphere left Jenny's senses reeling.

It also seemed odd that there were no other kids around, Jenny thought, listening to the solitary sounds of the little girl playing.

In the kitchen Steve puttered around, pouring them coffee after checking the mailbox outside. She padded to the island in the middle of the room.

"Steve?"

"Hmm?"

"Why doesn't Lola have any friends? She's playing alone in the backyard."

He placed the thick wad of envelopes on the bar, no doubt to deal with later. She had a sneaking suspicion more than a few were sympathy cards.

"Well, the psychologist thought it would place less stress on her. I lived here before I met Cara. I just—"

"But she should have friends. Children need someone to rely on, apart from the adults in her life. At the very least, an animal companion would be a start."

He frowned. "I didn't... It never occurred to me."

Steve turned to the fridge and started removing vegetables from the crisper then turned

back to the drawers in the island bench and pulled out the vegetable peeler.

He concentrated on dealing with the veggies for a moment before he put the peeler down with a clatter. "I'll think about it, okay?"

The whole situation felt like a daytime soap opera where the guy made dinner for the heroine right before he threw her out on her ear. The cup of coffee in front of her was cooling, and she shivered, knowing she had to make plans to leave...before he told her to go.

"Steve?"

He glanced at her with a questioning expression on his face. "I need to make plans to leave. I've imposed long enough."

He shook his head. "Actually, I want to talk to you about that. Later, after Lola goes to bed."

She looked at him steadily. "You know, I don't think that's a good idea."

She didn't want a replay of two nights ago. The guilt still gnawed at her gut even now.

Her fingers rubbed absently on a spot on the granite benchtop, helping her relieve the pressure that wound tightly within her.

Then he smiled and her stomach quivered in reaction. It took every ounce of control to tell her body he wasn't smiling at her...or at least not like that. He was just being friendly. Heat coiled inside her, and she felt her limbs loosening. Her nipples budded beneath the black dress, and she knew her panties had dampened in some kind of sick readiness for him.

For God's sake, Jenny! Don't be stupid. You're just horny after the excellent sex you had the other day. Don't go imagining fairytales though, because you know you're fat and frumpy. There is nothing about you he would want, except your skills as a psychologist.

She wanted to cry at her inner voice, but the brutal truth needed to be said, even if it was just in her mind. And yet, nothing could wipe away the memory of their bodies entwined.

The heat that had burned through her when he'd touched her had made her feel whole again. When he'd filled her to the hilt, stretched her most secret places even as he'd surged within, she'd felt beautiful and desired. Her breath caught again as her heart pounded hard against her rib cage.

Then she remembered his face when she'd shown him her wrists. The horror when he knew what she'd done. Anger had coiled through her initially, but now she wished she could take it back so he wouldn't know how broken she really was, that the Jenny he saw was nothing more than a façade.

"Jenny?"

The quietly spoken word woke her from the trance-like state she'd slipped into. She shook herself and looked back at him. "Sorry...you were saying?"

"Just that I think... As long as we stay away from alcohol, I think we should be okay." He smiled, and her heart tripped in her chest, remembering their actions from a couple of nights before.

She nodded abstractedly. "Okay. Promise me no more alcohol and I'm yours." She nearly died when she heard the words spring from her lips, but he smiled and winked.

"You're on." He turned toward the stove, and she dropped her head to her hands. He must think she was either a lunatic or a rampant nymphomaniac. Neither inspired any feelings of comfort in her.

Her phone beeped and she lifted her head and hunted in her pockets. It was a text from her boss. *Need you back – SOON. Work tomorrow?*

She sighed.

"Everything okay?" Steve's voice intruded on the sudden pit of despair she'd plunged into.

"My boss wants me back tomorrow. I need to..." The dread that pooled in her belly stopped her words. She didn't want to go back. She didn't want to leave Lola and Steve.

The dichotomy wasn't lost on her. Leave Steve and Lola behind? There really wasn't anything more than a tenuous, distant friendship. It wasn't like he loved her or had offered her a future. Her life was in Melbourne.

"Call him on the phone." He nodded to the handset on the wall. When she opened her mouth to argue, he pressed the point. "Don't fret about how much it'll cost. I can stand it. Go ring him and get some extra time."

She stared at him. Surely he couldn't be serious? There was no way she could afford take more time off work. She had bills to pay. And her boss would not be happy with her. While her boss understood her need for time off work, lately she had stretched the friendship a bit and he'd become difficult. Having to leave on the spot to deal with Cara... Well, after that he'd warned her he wouldn't tolerate any further interruptions to her work routine.

"Jenny?"

"I can't, Steve. I've got commitments...bills..."

"I'll cover them." He waved a hand in the air. "Look, I've got money. Resources. Let me help. Please?"

"I won't have a job to go back to." She was fully aware that no matter how badly he wanted to help, this was beyond the reach of the average man's wage. It was the point at which he would capitulate, she was sure.

Instead he smiled. "Do you really want to go back to that—to Melbourne and the constant cold weather and gray skies?"

If she were honest, Melbourne held no fond memories for her. She would prefer to move back to Queensland...reinvent herself...but it would be a leap of faith.

Perhaps it's time. You can be a new person. In that instant, she made a decision. "Yeah, you're right. I really don't want to go back."

He smiled. "Then go get Lola, send her for a bath, and make your call. I'll finish putting dinner together, and once she's in bed, I'll tell you my thoughts." He turned and she was left gaping after him.

STEVE SERVED THE STIR-FRIED VEGETABLES AND HOMEMADE fried rice in small bowls with cups

of refreshing green tea for himself and Jenny and milk for Lola. He'd thought about his argument ever since she'd told him about her job being in jeopardy. The way forward was clear in his mind.

Jenny had been quiet since she had come inside with Lola. The little girl had taken her hand and showed Jenny her Hello Kitty pajamas. Even after the months of silence from Lola, it still broke his heart that she wasn't sure enough of him to speak. He hoped Jenny could help her find the ability once more, so she could open up and enjoy all life had to offer. He needed to make the point to Lola that she was safe.

But was she really? They lived in a gated community, and his best friend was a police officer. Hell, he was an ex-policeman, for heaven's sake. She should be safe. Still, concern clawed at his insides. He'd thought Cara was safe too.

They ate in silence, and while he was lost in his own thoughts, it seemed so was Jenny. She remained quiet, a small crease between her eyes telling him she was thinking things over. Strange that after only a few days I'm already noticing these things. It wasn't like this with Cara. Then he reminded himself firmly that was unfair. They were different women, and Cara had been the love of his life, but the heat he'd expected to find in his personal tussle was absent.

During the entire meal, Lola watched them, a challenge in her eyes.

When they were done, the final clatter of cutlery on the plate, he realized he couldn't avoid talking to her. "Uh...Jenny? Why don't you make sure Lola brushes her teeth, then could you read her a book while I fill the dishwasher?"

"You cooked, and besides—" She stopped as he shook his head. "No. You go."

She bit her lip, and the action had something lurching deep inside his belly.

"I'm happy to clean up. You go on. I'm sure Lola would like someone else to read to her for a change, wouldn't you, Lola?" He needed time to prepare himself, and besides, it was clear Lola was accepting her by the way she took Jenny's hand.

She hadn't done anything quite like that with Cara, and the knowledge brought great discomfort.

The doorbell rang and he moved to the front of house and looked through the peephole. A courier stood on the steps, which surprised him, because couriers were usually buzzed onto the estate. He reached for the cricket bat he'd taken to keeping behind the heavy wooden front door. He wasn't taking any chances with Lola or Jenny's safety. They had to stay strong and healthy— alive—if they were going to solve this problem.

He jammed his foot behind the door, engaged the safety chain, and opened the door just enough to answer. "Yeah?"

"Ah...I have a delivery for you." The man sounded uncertain, and alarm bells rang in his head.

The sound of footsteps behind him had him turning involuntarily.

"Steve? Who is it?" When he heard Jenny's voice, the door swung open. Instantly, the man entered the room, and the door banged against the wall.

The man brushed past him, heading for Jenny. Steve's muscles seized.

"Bastard!" Steve swore as a splinter of wood from the smashed door hit him in the face. Pain exploded, and his concentration skittered away for a second, long enough for the courier thug to get his hands on Jenny.

She cried out and he blinked, catching sight of the man grappling with her. He moved now, adrenaline pumping, with his hands fisted. The bastard had his hands in her hair, and she twisted and turned, trying to escape. He pushed her toward the floor, and her cries of pain echoed through Steve's mind.

It propelled him and he reached out, grabbing the man's shoulders, his fingers digging deep. The man grunted, his grip on Jenny loosening as he turned to throw Steve off.

Steve wrenched the man away, and she sobbed as she fell to the floor with a loud thud. Red liquid splattered on the tiles.

Blood. Jenny had been hurt. He stood still as the man tore himself from his clutches, cloth tearing. In the back of Steve's mind came the order to run, catch the intruder as he retreated, but he couldn't make his body move. He stood as still as a statue. Everything took place in some kind of slow motion as his brain collected vital information. The details of the man's height, hair color, and the uniform he wore were filed away almost by instinct.

The sound of a car engine engaging snapped him out of his processing. His stomach roiled as the man fled out the door, and the sound of Jenny sobbing filled the air. Steve turned and stared at the red spots coating the tiles.

Jenny's hurt. He moved quickly, looking for the source of blood. She cowered on the floor, gripping her nose while it bled. A shaking hand covered her mouth, as if she were trying to contain the pain and fright.

"Jenny? Honey? Are you hurt anywhere else?" He couldn't control the panic in his voice. He wanted to soothe her. Hold her close. Tear the bastard apart limb by limb for daring to do this to her. Rage clawed at him as he accepted that he had stood still while the man had fled. He was some amazing kind of wimp, he told himself furiously.

"He...he was going to hurt me, and I don't know why."

The broken words shattered him as much as her actions when she crawled into his arms. The mass in his stomach congealed. Tears traced down her cheeks, mixing with the blood on her face, and he moaned slightly.

"Oh God, Jenny, let me see."

Instead she turned away. He couldn't blame her. What had happened to him? Why hadn't he reacted? Saved her from injury? He'd failed her...just as he'd failed Cara.

A sound from the hallway caught his attention and he whipped around. Lola stood backed up against the wall, her little face white and drawn. His mind told him she was shrinking away from the violence, not him.

He took a step in her direction, but she slunk over to Jenny. He watched as she moved Jenny's hands away from her face. Jenny stayed still under the careful touches of the little girl, and finally he knew... She'd seen this kind of injury before. He'd felt ill before, now he was sure he would retch on the floor. No child should have to experience this.

Jenny took the child's hand and rose slowly. Without a word, she led Lola away from the scene of the assault, and Steve stood leaning against the wall for support.

There and then he vowed to find the people who had done this. To nail them in a court of law and make sure they paid for their crimes to Jenny...to Lola.

Jenny led Lola toward the bedroom. Her nose and mouth throbbed. She'd seen the look of naked rage on Steve's face. She'd felt his hands shake against her as he'd made a silent inspection of her injuries.

No man had ever done something like that for her before. She didn't know how she should feel. Wounded, yes, but lost and floundering in a sea of disbelief too.

Lola opened the door to the en-suite and Jenny understood instantly that she'd experienced this behavior before. It made sense.

Mutism was frequently caused by a trauma. She was distrustful and wary. Everything came together and Jenny wanted to bundle the girl up in her arms. Instead she waited, cautious until Lola allowed her nearer.

"Lola? Can you help me?"

She gazed at Jenny, her features pale in the artificial light.

"I need a face washer, so I can clean up." Her mouth and nose ached, and talking clearly and slowly didn't help. Each movement jarred injured flesh, but it was necessary and soothing for both of them.

The girl nodded and turned, padding into the bedroom. Jenny heard the sound of wood scraping as Lola opened and closed drawers. Waiting was difficult, but she refused to rush the child, either with the chore or emotionally. So Jenny waited in silence.

The door opened and Lola edged into the tiny room, handing her a washer. Jenny reached for the tap, but Lola's hand was there first, turning on the cold water. Jenny thrust the cloth under the running tap then wrung it out and wiped the blood away, her mind only half on the task.

A range of possible therapies rolled while her heart ached for the little girl, and Jenny nearly cried when the truth hit her. Lola was almost as damaged as she was. The child had a long road ahead, and Jenny felt a bond with her that overrode the last vestiges of guilt at not returning to Melbourne. Lola needed her more than any other patient she had ever worked with.

On a sigh, Jenny focused her attention on her reflection in the mirror.

Her face was white as she stripped down to her plain cotton panties and bra. Lola watched her silently. The dress fell to the floor and she grimaced down at it. "I'll deal with that later."

For the first time in a long while, she didn't feel embarrassed that anyone saw her, or the flesh she usually tried to cover up.

"Come on. I need to find some clean clothes."

The child nodded and followed her to the bedroom. Jenny opened the wardrobe, spying a pair of track pants and top. She snatched them from the hanger and pulled them on.

"Right, Miss Lola, come with me and I'll get you some warm milk. Would that help you sleep?"

The child gazed at her steadily.

Jenny crouched down to the child's level so she could look into her eyes. "You know this isn't your fault, don't you? It's bad men making bad decisions." She slid shaking fingers through the little girl's hair, pushing it back off her face. "They do things to hurt people who have done nothing wrong because they can." She emphasized the point with another soft touch on her cheek. "Steve won't let anything happen to you. You're safe."

Lola nodded silently, as if still unsure, and Jenny's heart nearly broke.

She lifted the child into her arms and carried her down the hall, all the while reinforcing her message. "You did the right thing by staying out of the way until he was gone. I'm so glad you weren't hurt."

The girl smiled; a tiny tremble of her lower lip.

Jenny's eyes misted. She blinked quickly and cleared her throat. "I'm going to make you some warm milk, and you can sit in my lap while I read you another story. Okay?"

Lola nodded again.

Steve waited for them at the end of the hall. "Are you both okay?"

Jenny nodded, but could see he was still upset. Right now, Lola was her priority. "I'm going to make Lola a warm drink and then we'll read a book."

"I rang Dave. He's going to pop around and check for fingerprints. He'll probably want to talk to you."

She nodded. "I kind of expected that, but Miss Lola and I have a date."

She snuggled Lola close and padded into the kitchen, popping her onto a chair.

"You know, Lola, I used to like warm milk when I was your age. My mother would put a

little vanilla and sugar into it. Have you ever tried it like that?" Lola shook her head.

"Well then, there's no time like the present, is there?" Jenny snatched a small pot from the cupboard, then milk and vanilla from the fridge. A quick rattle around the pantry netted her some granulated sugar, and she carefully poured the amounts, relying on memory.

As she stirred the milk, Jenny talked to the little girl, picking ridiculous, but non- threatening topics, from how she'd seen the fashion runway display in the middle of Melbourne to the silly joke she had got in an email.

Once the drinks were poured and Lola was back in her lap, she finally relaxed, drank the warm milk, and nuzzled up. Jenny reached for one of the books in a holder on the kitchen benchtop, and settled into the repetitive and rhyming story.

By the time they got halfway through the book, Lola was dozing lightly against Jenny's chest, and she carefully pushed the hair from her dear little face. "Oh, Lola...What on earth are we going to do?"

She looked up as Steve popped his head around the doorway to the kitchen. "Everything okay?" he whispered.

She nodded.

He frowned. "Should we put her to bed?"

"In a few minutes. Let's wait just a bit longer."

He nodded and entered the room.

"Come and sit down. I want her well and truly settled before we carry her to bed. She's already been through enough tonight. While she's sleeping so well, I don't want to risk her waking up."

"Dave's been and gone. He'll pop by in the morning to talk to you."

"Okay."

Jenny closed her eyes and let her mind think through the episode. Steve had pulled the

man away as he started to punch her, so his fist hadn't connected as hard as she expected, but Steve had clearly been horrified afterward. She'd seen him stop as if frozen in place. The look on his face would probably haunt her for a long time.

It was something she had seen before on the faces of families of assault victims. Until now, she hadn't quite understood the trauma they experienced. *I need to let him know it's not his fault.* Here and now, with Lola on her lap, wasn't the time though.

So she waited, listening to the tick-tock of the clock from the corner of the living room until she was sure Lola was sleeping deeply enough to not notice the movement. Carefully, she rose with the child clasped against her, then made her way to the bedroom. Once there, Steve slid the sheet back so she could slip the little girl into her bed and tuck her in.

Steve retreated to the doorway, watching and blocking the glow of light from the hall.

"Good night, sweetheart." She couldn't resist gently smoothing a hand over Lola's brow before she backed away.

Steve's hand reached out for hers, and with a shiver, she accepted it. Together they moved to the lounge.

"How are you feeling?" His eyes scanned her face and soft fingers rose to touch the area that hurt the most.

"I've felt better." She wanted to make light of the situation, but she just didn't have the heart for it.

He leaned in and dropped a kiss between her brows. "I'm so sorry. I didn't stop him hurting you." He leaned back, and she gave a tiny sigh.

"You couldn't stop him. What you did do was pull him away so his punch wasn't so hard." She inhaled and his scent filled her senses. "You can't own what someone else does, you know that."

"But I should have—"

She stopped his bitter recriminations with a finger against his lips. "No, you couldn't. You did what you could and then you stopped." There was stark pain in his features now. It hurt to say the words, but she refused to shy away from the truth. "I know you're struggling with that, but you stopped him from hurting me as much as he wanted to. You pulled him away and stopped his attack. You scared him and he ran away. That makes you my hero."

His bark of laughter contained no mirth. "Oh, right. The hero who stands by and watches a woman get beat up. Some hero."

"No, don't say that. You saved me...that's what counts."

He stepped back, his usual graceful gait unsteady. "We need to talk." "Yes, we do, because I think I know what caused Lola to stop talking."

# CHAPTER SEVEN

They sat in the deeply padded seats where they'd sat a mere two nights before. The wine- red leather was cool and squishy, and Jenny had to stop herself from cuddling down into it. Her body ached, and the shape of the chair molded around her.

Steve placed a glass of soda water beside her on a coaster. She thanked him and waited for him to settle to whatever it was he felt he needed to discuss.

"So...you said you think you know..." He waved his hand in the air, and she watched, mesmerized. "Jenny?"

"Oh! Well, I can't be one-hundred percent sure just yet, but based on the way Lola reacted tonight, I believe she has seen previous assaults. She was calm—too calm under the circumstance. I would say it's as if she's been in this situation before." Jenny lifted the glass to her lips and sipped. "This may be a gut reaction, but I don't think I'm too far off the mark."

He nodded. "I see."

"Steve, I don't know that any kind of treatment will be fast. In order to be successful, it's going to take time. She'll need to form a bond with her psychologist before they can really commence any kind of therapy. Even then, it's going to almost need to be play-based or art- based, so she doesn't feel strained or—"

"Or pushed. Yes, I see where you're going."

Jenny slumped further back into her seat, her gaze settling on the photographs on the wall. "She's going to need a steady hand...someone who's willing to go the whole way with her. I wouldn't be surprised if she doesn't also have a problem with abandonment too, given the loss of Cara and whatever happened to her parents and family."

He picked up the glass and sloshed it around while frowning down at the iced tea. "That's what I wanted to talk to you about. I'd like you to stay, to take on her therapy."

She'd expected this, but it wasn't something she should do. The oath she had taken wasn't something she'd set aside easily. But they needed to find an answer and quickly. The people certainly weren't giving up anytime soon, that much was obvious.

"I shouldn't. I mean, Lola is almost Cara's daughter. It feels wrong..." But the thought of how long it could take for Lola to become comfortable with someone else was a concern.

"We don't have time, surely you understand that." It was as if he'd read her mind.

She bit her lip and turned away. "I couldn't—"

"No. It has to be you. You're the only one we can trust right now."

The truth of his words speared her. The longer she quibbled, the longer it would take to get to the bottom of Lola's issues. And in the meantime, they might hurt Lola. Or Steve.

The thought left her shivering. She couldn't let that happen. "Okay, but only until we can find out what happened, then I must hand it over to another psychologist."

He nodded and sipped again on the drink. "We also need to talk about—"

Her head snapped up. "No, we don't." Her cold words were

aimed at shutting down the situation, but he sat back in the seat gazing at her.

"We do. Otherwise we'll be walking around each other, wondering how to cope with this thing between us."

She gulped. As much as she wanted to avoid it, he wasn't going to let her. And he was right. It needed to be resolved.

"All right then, what did you want to say?" She steeled herself, fingers gripping the arms of the chair now that she had put down the drink.

He blushed, and she grinned just a little bit at his discomfort. "It was an accident, a case

of losing our inhibitions and trying to deal with our grief."

Watching him, it was clear he'd been practicing the words all night. "So it was just an accident? Unintentional, and will never happen again?"

Steve opened his mouth, and Jenny waited for the confirmation, but it didn't come. His face clouded and he looked away.

Something warm settled in her chest, and a fascination rose in her. Could it be? No, he

couldn't possibly want her, and besides, Cara was firmly between them.

"I can't promise that." His low words startled her.

"Look, Steve. seriously, you don't want me. I'm so messed up I don't know up from down, and I already have enough hang-ups to carry around with me. You wouldn't want someone with that level of issues pulling you down." She said the words quietly. "And I'm not the kind of woman you would want or need by your side." She smiled, trying vainly to hide the pain in her words.

He frowned. "Jenny...you are..."

"I'm large, and I'm not the woman of your dreams. We buried her today." Oh God! How those words hurt, but they had to be said. Steve was one more thing she couldn't have.

His face darkened, and she wondered if she'd been a little too brutal. She stood as he did, ready to leave the room, but he moved toward her.

"Why? Why do you put yourself down like that?" His words bit as surely as the grip of his fingers on her upper arms.

"It's the truth. Sure, the truth hurts, but I won't hide from—"

His mouth crashed down on hers, silencing her harsh answer, and his tongue demanded entry. Entry she couldn't deny him. It swept within the cavern of her mouth and she could taste him—delicious, dangerous, all man.

She pulled away. "You shouldn't—"

"I can, and I will. You're beautiful, Jenny. I watched you today with Lola, how kind and loving you were. Soft when she needed it, and firm too when it called for that." His large hands framed her face, and she nuzzled closer to feel the warmth of his touch on her skin.

Her body yearned for him. Her nipples swelled and her breasts engorged. Her panties grew wet, and she pressed her legs together as the instant arousal burned her. "Don't do this, Steve."

She whispered the words, and yet he still dipped his head toward her mouth again.

"I can't help myself. You're like an intoxicating drug." His lips found hers, and this time the touch was gentle.

Her frustrations and concerned fizzled away. They could talk tomorrow, when there wasn't need pooling inside them both.

Instead of words, he gave her slow touches and caresses. He drugged her with the feel of his fingertips as he brushed the hair from her face then traced her brows before dipping to her lips. His fingers trailed over the side of jaw. She arched her neck and swallowed as his thumb settled to her lower lip, the tiniest pressure destroying her with subtle eroticism.

She clung to Steve's shoulders, her lips opened, and she flicked her tongue over the pad of his finger. He hissed, jerked, and stilled for a moment. Their gazes meshed...held...then his evocative exploration continued.

His hand moved down her neck, tracing her collarbone, then

slipped down her arm. His eyes burned a path where he touched, and she yearned for more.

Dear heavens! He was barely touching her and she was so aroused!

He backed her against the wall, and once his fingers found hers, he linked them and pulled away from her. She frowned as he lifted their twined hands above her head.

"You're exquisite, Jenny. I adore the way your breasts draw my eyes. Your arse is round and full, just right for my hands to touch and knead," he whispered.

She shivered under his touch. He let go of her hands, and she started to lower them. "No...leave them there."

His hands sought the zipper closure of her track top, dragging it down slowly, and she melted before he released the cloth. The top gaped open and she knew he could see her utilitarian bra. She also wasn't small or pert. He laid a shaking finger against her beaded nipple through the cotton lycra fabric.

"Your skin is so pale, your nipples look like ripe strawberries set in the most exquisite cream."

His words seduced her as effectively as his touch, and she couldn't help herself, dropping her arms and covering his hand as it continued exploring her dips and hollows, her hips moving in an unconscious rhythm.

"Steve?" She needed to know where this was going.

He drew back slightly. "Jenny...tonight will you choose to stay with me? With no alcohol? No inducements? Just two lonely people who want each other?" His husky words stilled her movements.

Was this what she wanted? Did she want to sleep with this man? Enjoy his body for as long as he wanted her?

She gripped his hand and pulled it away from her breast.

"Yes."

With slow, careful movements, he drew her down the hall past Lola's room. This time he opened the door to a room she hadn't entered. Only dimly did she note the chocolate tones of the comforter, the pale walls. He turned on a bedside lamp and carefully watched her as he shucked his clothes.

"I'm going to touch you all over. Kiss every inch of your beautiful skin. Then I'm going to fill you, and when you cry out, I'm going to suck you dry before I love you again." His eyes glittered, and his face was drawn with desire.

His pants slipped to the floor and his underwear followed. Her mouth dried and her fingers curled, itching to run over the skin he'd uncovered.

The heat in her belly flared higher and hotter, and the skin of her pussy lips quivered. She lifted shaking fingers to push away her top but he was there once more. Gloriously naked, with his erection jutting from between his legs. A line of dark hair trailed down from his navel to join with the thickly curled hairs that did nothing to hide just how aroused he was.

His muscles moved in the light, and she gasped, noting the strength in his body she had barely seen before.

The material of her top fluttered to the floor and his arms wound around her, his fingers searching for the clasp of her bra. He breathed heavily, and she wanted his lips against hers. Jenny gathered all her determination, rose to her tiptoes, and laid her open lips against his. This time his mouth devoured hers, his whiskers rasping the skin of her face as their tongues danced.

Her bra released and her breasts sagged, but she didn't care as his hands burrowed beneath the cotton, molding themselves over the heavy globes. His thumbs flicked, and she pulled away, arching and crying out. "Steve?"

"For me. All for me." With a savage jerk, he pulled the straps from her and the bra went sailing over his head.

The primal need in his eyes matched the hunger within her. His fingers tugged at the band of her pants and found the panties below. He forced them down with a jerky motion, all the vestiges of civility stripped from them both as they groped at each other, desire flashing between them.

She stepped from the clothes, and his hands firmed, kneading her flesh. She gasped as a finger traced from her arse to her damply ready intimate folds.

When he dipped a hard, questing finger inside her, she moaned and shook. Her body tightened. She was so very ready for his invasion.

"Steve. The bed..." She hissed the words, and he laughed savagely.

"Not yet." His words left her senses reeling.

What more... Rational thought fled as he kissed her deeply, his passion possessing her completely.

As the thought began he moved, slowly slipping down her body while he searched every

inch of her skin with his lips and tongue. He found one breast, suckled for a moment, then shifted to the other.

"Oh God, Steve. More!" Her demand was almost soundless.

He continued licking and nibbling as he traversed her body. He stopped at her rounded belly, dipping his tongue into her indented navel. Her thighs shook and she panted, hungry for oxygen and more of the exquisite torture. When his tongue drew circles around the dent, she flamed hotter than ever before. The burning sensation below the touch of his finger stole every thought while he continued the light, thrusting movements between her legs.

He dipped further, pulling his finger from within her. When he licked his finger, her legs nearly gave way at the carnality of his actions.

He reached out, using the wet finger he'd just enjoyed to part her folds. "So beautiful."

He toyed for an instant with the nub of her clit and flicked it with his tongue. Jenny thrashed, lost in the hazy world she'd never experienced before. Never like this.

He placed his mouth over her mound, the sweet heat tearing a moan from her throat. He suckled her intimately, and she shook and shivered.

"No more. Oh, please, Steve...No more!" Blindly, she pulled at him, dragging him back up her body.

Their lips met and clung. The taste of her essence on his mouth surprised her. The musky tang added to the danger of his touch. Together, they shuffled to the bed and fell upon it, the mattress see-sawing under their combined weights.

Hands moved urgently as she cupped the weight of his balls, testing the fullness, then her fingers wandered over his erection. It was hot and silky, yet firm beneath her touch. She found the slit at the tip and felt the dampness that leaked from it. He was as turned on as she was.

His fingers fondled between her legs and at her breasts. She opened her legs wide, showing him wordlessly just how ready she was for him. He looked down, holding himself still against her.

"Last chance." He breathed heavily and she knew what he needed to know.

She glanced down, saw they had reached the point of no return, and threw caution to the wind. "I want this. I want you inside me. I want to feel the burn."

His mouth descended, tongues mating as he slipped inside her. His movements were slow, undulating, and she met his thrusts as her hands roamed over his back, scoring his flesh, branding him hers.

The fever built, each move ratcheting her higher and tighter until all that remained was the hunger and desire. He groaned against her mouth as she gasped, feeling him fill her all the way.

Jenny arched, her fingers gripping tightly at his hips as he pushed himself a little further in, seeking release. When it came, the orgasm was strong. It buzzed through her veins. She gave herself up to the sensations, her womb tightening rhythmically.

He grunted, thrusted one last time, and his body convulsed in her arms, finding release. Deep within she felt the jetting of his seed, and she loved it. Every minute detail shone with crystalline clarity.

He held still against her. Then slowly he moved to lie beside her in the darkness, his arm gathering her close. Their harsh breathing calmed and they dozed.

STEVE WOKE GRADUALLY, LETTING HIS BODY CLIMB THROUGH the layers of wellbeing that wrapped around his consciousness. The feel of a warm, curvy body snuggled close beside him confused him for just an instant before he realized it was Jenny. She lay there naked against his nude form.

He turned, and she scooted away slightly. He frowned and looked into her face. She was deeply asleep, but the action worried him. Even in sleep, after their amazing bout of lovemaking, she pulled away.

He didn't like that at all. It spoke of problems he didn't know about or understand. He lay back, letting his arm rest over his eyes while he considered the problem.

Someone was after Lola, because she knew something. Someone had killed Cara, and it seemed safe to assume it was something to do with the threat to Lola.

Someone had hurt Jenny, and for a moment, the fear ballooned within him, until he heard her softly snuffling in her sleep.

Jenny...generous, loving, and lonely Jenny, beautiful Jenny, who'd given him all her passion, not holding anything back. At the edge of his conscience the thought that she meant more to him raised its head. Fear had him slamming the lid on any thoughts like that. Remember Cara!

He frowned. They'd both wanted this connection, but it wounded him that Jenny had withdrawn from him, even uncon-sciously. He guessed it had more to do with her past than their mutual feelings of betrayal to Cara. That he couldn't do a damn thing about it bothered him even further.

Each time he and Jenny made love—had sex, he corrected himself

—the bond between them grew. Each taste and touch left him wanting more.

He thought back to her words that had stung him, propelling him into the action that had led to the wonderful intimacy they'd shared. *I'm large, and I'm not the woman of your dreams. We buried her today.* He still felt as if he'd betrayed Cara with each kiss, each teasing touch, and each choice he made, yet the guilt didn't have the depth it had the first time.

The knowledge that Cara may as well have been lying in the bed between them right now, along with the memory that they'd just buried her, made him feel sick—for both himself and Jenny.

He mourned Cara's loss, he told himself. She'd been a bright flame in his life, but now she was gone...dead.

He forced his mind from the negative thoughts that swirled around. He needed to make his offer to Jenny, the one that would keep her there for Lola.

Liar! His mind screamed that he wanted more than help for Lola, but he steadfastly refused to consider that. The thoughts chased around in his mind, leaving him even more confused and frustrated.

He tossed and turned, and Jenny half-roused.

"What...where?"

Her husky voice aroused him once more. His penis started to swell, and his heart rate sped up. *How on earth can I want her again so soon?* But he did. He wanted everything she had to offer.

Jenny moved slowly, the sheet dropping closer to the curve of her breast. "Steve?" Her breathy enquiry was little more than a sigh of half-awareness. Her eyelids fluttered closed again as she drifted back off to sleep.

A seed of devilry entered his mind. Carefully, he peeled the sheet from her body where she had pulled them up around her gorgeous, lush form. Her pale skin shone in the dim light, and he let his gaze travel over her. He had suckled both those breasts, enjoying the plump bounty. He realized that skinny women really didn't appeal to him. He much preferred to have something to touch and hold onto.

Steve's gaze rolled down her body, finding the indentation of her waist, her rounded tummy and navel. His inspection continued downward, while his fingers teased the thatch of hair at the entrance to her hot, moist core. The one he'd recently filled and fitted around him like a glove. Just thinking about slipping into her heated his body, he had to suppress a groan.

He reached over, found the pink bud of her nipple, and lightly touched it with the pad of one finger. It sprang back, distending under his touch. He pressed it again, just a little harder, and she shifted, moving slightly so that her legs widened.

His mouth dried. How far could he go before she woke fully? He smiled. It was time to find out just how she reacted to his touches on an instinctive level.

Steve levered himself up so that her nipple was below his mouth, and he gently blew. She moaned in her sleep, and he plumped her breast in his free hand, opened his mouth, and took the distended berry into it. He sucked as her hips moved, and when he released her nipple, she reacted to his touch without thinking about it. That pleased him...enormously.

He slid his hand down her body, exploring soft curves all over again. He loved the feeling of her rounded belly and ran light fingers over her warm flesh. For a moment a flash of what she would look like full and large with child—his child—filled his mind, and he gulped before shying away from that thought. Instead, he tracked his fingers further downward toward her hidden folds.

He found the hair that hid her core and gently ran his fingers through it. They were soft against his palm, and he hissed as his erection jerked with need.

On a moan, Jenny moved again, her hips arching unconsciously, and he slipped one finger inside her hot, wet sheath. He rubbed as she writhed. He dipped his mouth down over her moist core, the tip of his tongue touched her, and he delighted in her taste, rich and musky. Far better than the finest wine he'd ever consumed. His finger moved back and forth, and she rolled slightly, as if encouraging him to find the right spot.

He sat up, settling his mouth over hers, rapaciously feeding on the taste of her lips.

Her arms rose, even as she remained cocooned in her dreams, folding around him while her tongue dipped within his mouth in a parody of the connection his body craved. He positioned himself and slid home, filling her so slowly he tensed. He wasn't certain how long he could hold on, but was determined to feel the sensation of orgasm rippling throughout her body first.

He grunted and pulled away. Her fingers tangled in his hair, tugging him back, but he laughed and pulled further away. "Sleeping Beauty, this is your punishment for tempting me." She woke with a thready cry as he pushed back harder, and her thighs tightened like a vise against his buttocks, the rhythmic clenching leaving him gritting his teeth as he arched and undulated.

God, he loved the taste and feel of this woman. He loved how she filled him with heat and need.

He gave one last thrust, unable to help himself, and she cried out. Her climax came quickly and surprised him. The milking sensation so strong it pushed him over the edge. He let go and spilled himself deeply within her body. "Jenny!"

He held himself still, his heart beating wildly in his chest. How could this happen? How could things get so out of hand? The familiar confusion he'd felt since meeting Jenny beat down on him again. He pulled back emotionally, and saw on her face the moment she realized it as well. The dawning horror on her face gutted him.

# CHAPTER EIGHT

Jenny lay still. Steve was still seated within her, hard and hot, but she saw on his face a distance that chilled her to the bone. They'd had sex, again...unprotected, wild sex, just as they had done every time. It was worse now, because it was the second time on the night after he'd buried his lover.

So what on earth does that make me? Easy? She nearly choked on the thought.

Jenny tried to pull away, but he gripped her hands and kept her still. "Jenny, I need to talk to you."

Oh yes, just the words a girl wants to hear right after a man has finished screwing her.

The bitter thoughts hurt to the very depths of her soul, but she needed to face reality.

Hot, burning tears welled in her eyes, and bile rose in her throat.

The first time was bad enough, but she'd reasoned it was two drunken people needing closure after they had lost someone they were both close to.

The second was consensual. Maybe not the right thing to do under the circumstances, but they'd both agreed to the intimacy.

Since he'd started right after she'd told him what she thought of his so-called interest...maybe that made it a pity fuck. Her shoulders slumped.

The third... She closed her eyes, hating the truth that left her shaking.

"Jenny? Honey, don't do this." His words entreated and she pulled away, feeling his penis slip from between her legs. She felt the emptiness, but had to get away. Had to go now! If she stayed...

The truth was, if she stayed, they would do this again and again. No matter how rational her brain might be, her body wanted him. Wanted him to fill her, pleasure her. She would keep fooling herself that something real and lasting could form between them.

A bubble of pain erupted, and she clapped her hand to her mouth, desperate to stop the sound.

"Jenny, please...listen to me." His hands caught hers, but she tugged away. "Look at me!" The growling tone demanded she do so, and her body betrayed her yet again as she saw the hard planes of his face, the tight lines of strain around his eyes and mouth.

"Don't..." She whispered the word, hoping he'd hear the guilt and let her go.

"Oh, baby, don't do this. I want you. I want this."

He leaned forward, and she knew he believed the words at this moment, but they weren't real. These emotions were ghosts of what they both wanted. It was the stress causing him to see a connection where none existed between them except for sexual compatibility. Her rational brain wanted to quote from some textbook, to show him that what he felt was...ephemeral.

The emotions he felt were little more than his mind working to find a solution to his pain. She couldn't bring herself to say the words though. If she did, he'd turn away from her, and she'd be gutted.

"Jenny? Talk to me." His voice pleaded, and the pain consumed her. Black clouds of despair filled her chest.

"I can't..." She gasped the words out.

He shook her slightly. "Dammit, Jenny! I'm trying to tell you I feel something strong for you. I don't understand it yet, but I want to."

The words intruded on the cloud of loss, sorrow, and fear that surrounded her. She dismissed them. It was grief talking. It had to be. She clung to her denial.

If he meant them, they were in trouble, because she was drawn to this man, and she didn't think there was any way she could cope if he made her believe it and then left her. Just like everyone else had done in the past.

"No. What you feel is survivor's guilt wrapped up in some kind of..." She waved her hands in the air, searching for the right words while her heart beat wildly in her chest. She pulled away, clambering to the side of the bed. "What we feel right now isn't love. It's lust and the need to prove we're alive."

"God damn it, Jenny! I'm being honest here." His voice echoed with frustration and anger.

She raised a hand. "Look, we've been under great emotional stress. What you're feeling...it's got no depth. It's. Not. Real." She nodded, thankful her voice didn't crack or break as she gave her pronouncement.

He groaned. "I know you're the psychologist, but this is real. What I feel for you is real. I've never experienced this before. It's like heaven and hell."

She closed her eyes, wishing she could block her hearing too. God, how she wanted to believe his words. They tantalized and gave her a glimpse of a future with this strong man by her side, Lola with them, but it was fantasy...nothing more. "Steve..."

He put a soft finger to her lips. "I don't know how to prove it to you, but give me a chance. Please?"

Her body quaked. Could she do this? Could she give him the chance he asked for? Was she strong enough?

"I don't..." Her resolve weakened. *What if it is real? Will I let my fears strip my one chance of happiness away?* She looked down at the white scars on her wrists. *Will I succumb to the blackness again if it* isn't real? Can I afford to take the chance on missing out on a love that could last forever? The jumble of thoughts argued and warred in her head.

"Please." His soft entreaty broke through the wall around her heart. But instead, she shook her head, and left him on the bed.

THIS TIME WHEN STEVE WOKE, HE WAS ALONE. HIS HAND traced the indentation of her head on his pillow. "Why did you leave, Jenny?"

A wall of reserve had frozen him out. Not for the first time, he wondered why she was so gun-shy. He knew she had issues with her size, though the generous curves of hips and breasts attracted him more than he ever thought they would.

In her eyes, there was a distant and long-seated pain. "Who hurt you?"

He slumped back to the bed. He'd already learned she was giving, caring, and dedicated—just look at the way she worried about Lola.

He dragged his hands over his tired eyes and scrubbed, hoping to wipe away the confusion that had taken up residence in his head.

Jenny. Cara. Two women, vastly different, yet close. Cara had told him once that they had grown up together. Attended the same schools, until Cara went to the private college her parents had sent her to for a short while. Funny, he'd never thought to enquire why. It hadn't seemed important.

He shrugged. It wasn't important now either. Except...apart from Jenny, no friends of Cara's had attended her funeral. He'd never met any. Cara had always insisted there was time. She'd been wrong, on so many fronts.

"Dammit, Cara, why do I suddenly realize you're an enigma? Why didn't I push harder to know more about you?"

A flash of insight answered his query. Because Cara had always shrugged it off, as if she didn't really want him to know the real woman. The thought gave him pause, and he felt a shuddering sigh escape, the sound unsteady.

He pulled the sheet away and stood, his skin caressed by the cool current wafting from the air-conditioning, feathering his body, just as Jenny's touch had. Jenny.

She carried her troubles locked inside herself. It seemed to him she was scared to face what grew between them. Could it be she was as mixed up about it as he was?

"I don't want to hurt her." He didn't. He wanted something more than just the satisfaction of pleasuring her.

With a sudden jerk, he pulled open the wardrobe drawer, scanning his clothes with blind eyes. She'd been up for a while because the bed was cold. Steve was intent on making the most of every moment with her. Learn what drove her, what had wounded her, and how to heal her.

A nagging presentiment told him he'd only have one chance with Jenny. Make it work or lose it. The thought left his stomach plummeting again.

JENNY NEEDED TIME TO THINK, BUT SHE DOUBTED STEVE WOULD give her that. Her mind was still whirling at the memory of his words. How in hell was she supposed to concentrate knowing that he labored under the impression that there was a possibility of some kind of relationship?

Jenny showered quickly. Even though she'd retreated to her bedroom last night, after dragging her clothes back over her sex-spent body, she hadn't bathed, instead seeking the oblivion of sleep.

She'd told herself it was as much for the sake of propriety that she hadn't wandered through the house naked. After all, she'd had to consider Lola. It hadn't felt right. She didn't want the little girl to think that it was okay to hop into another person's bed whenever something bad happened.

She rinsed the shampoo from her hair, slicking it back off her face with savage movements. Jenny turned off the taps and stepped out of the shower, grabbing one of the fluffy towels.

Today she needed to go through Cara's bag. She'd only found the clothing the undertaker required then closed it again. Since then, she'd carefully avoided looking at it.

It was time to address what she'd ignored, so perhaps she could find a way of dealing with her grief and building a new life...one without Cara in it.

She shook her head when she questioned if Steve and Lola would be part of it.

She sighed. Clearing the apartment wasn't something she looked forward to. The same with sorting out her other affairs. Did she have a solicitor? Was there a will, and who would make those arrangements?

"That's Steve's job, you idiot." She scowled at herself in the mirror.

The whole mess still felt very odd. She didn't want it to be real. Emotions swamped her again. If she hadn't known better, hadn't seen the body, she would have called the situation a cruel hoax.

Pulling on fresh underwear, she grimaced, thinking of what Steve had done down there. Ohmygosh! He'd seen the stretch marks, and said nothing. She bit her lip, embarrassed by what he'd seen.

She grabbed a basic white bra and fastened it, then rifled through the wardrobe looking for something that flattered her large figure. She hunted through the clothing options before settling on bootleg jeans, a loose, white peasant blouse, and boots. Jenny found a hair clip and she tied her hair back off her face. She could go the whole hog and slap on makeup, but she shrugged. He'd seen her at her worst, and makeup wouldn't fix the major issues she had.

She caught sight of Cara's bag laying on the floor and she nearly reached for it, but a tap at the door had her inwardly sighing. "Come in," she called out.

The door opened, and Steve stood there staring at her. "Jenny? Want a coffee?"

His voice warmed her, and she had a vision of him, naked and leaning over her, that voice telling her what he planned to do to her. She couldn't open Cara's bag now. It felt wrong.

With a humph she backed away from the bag. "Yeah, I'm on my way."

She hurried down the corridor, following him until she reached Lola's room. She peered within, but the little girl was nowhere to be seen. Jenny headed for the kitchen.

"Hey, where's..." Her voice trailed away as she saw the little girl with tousled hair and pink cheeks smiling at her.

Jenny returned the grin.

"Lola just got up." Steve slipped the coffee into her hands, their fingers touching for a second longer than necessary, and a spark of electricity filled her. "So we should organize breakfast and then decide what we're going to do with the rest of our day." He glanced at the pile of white envelopes and picked them up.

"I can deal with that, if you'd like?" she offered.

He stared at her then shook his head. "No. I really should." He flipped through the envelopes, then stopped and stared at one of them. "Do you know who she used for her solicitor?"

He looked at her and Jenny shrugged. "It's probably the same firm her parents used. Um, Chalmers and something?"

He laid the rest of the envelopes on the benchtop, tugging at the lip of the envelope still in his hands, and then he walked around the bench and dropped himself heavily into the last seat. "I don't think I'm ready for this." He wiped a shaking hand over his face, and she longed to reach out and smooth the worries away.

"Whether you're ready for it or not, it'll still need doing."

His glance at her was resigned. "I know."

She reached out, briefly touching his hand, wanting only to give him comfort. "How about you drop me at her place and I start packing up her clothes? I can take her bag with me to make it easier."

The girl beside her wiggled and gave an angry growl.

Jenny glanced down, surprised at the change in the girl's demeanor. "It's okay, Lola. She won't ever leave you..."

The girl wriggled more, and for the first time, she wondered about Lola's time with Cara. "Lola!" Steve's voice was tight, not at all the tone he usually used with the child.

"This isn't characteristic?"

He shook his head. "No. I don't know what—"

Jenny caught Steve's attention with a carefully aimed kick and looked at him meaningfully. He turned toward her, startled, and must have seen the look in her eye as he closed his mouth.

"You know what, Lola?" Jenny turned back to the little girl with a falsely bright smile. "Why don't you go get dressed, and we'll think of something else we could do today?"

Lola sat still for an instant longer and then slowly moved. It hurt to watch the withdrawal on her face, but she kept her mouth shut until Lola left the room.

"Oh, Steve, there's something wrong. The minute I suggested going over to Cara's, she started acting..." She searched her brain for a word, but the process had turned to a treacle-like consistency, slow and thick. "I don't know...weird? You saw it, didn't you?"

He nodded slowly. "Yes, she always seemed reluctant to go home with Cara, but I put it down to wanting us to be together."

Jenny absently massaged the ache between her brows, while she thought over the child's reaction. "Whatever caused her silence, it could have taken place somewhere around there."

Steve looked at her, his gaze thoughtful. "That never occurred to me." His face paled. "God! The times I've bribed her or got a little cross..." His voice trailed away. "Do you think that's really the case?"

"It's just a feeling, but I would pretty much bet that somewhere in the vicinity of Cara's place is where something big and traumatic occurred in Lola's life. Was there any evidence of...anything bad there?"

"Look, where Cara lived...it's not the best part of town for kids. I didn't like her living there, but she laughed it off, saying she was a grown woman and more than capable of looking after herself." He nodded, accepting her professional opinion. "Okay, so what do we do now?" He sighed.

"I don't know. Is there someone you trust who she would be comfortable staying with?"

"Dave...he and his girlfriend, Fiona, have babysat her a couple of times. Usually here, so they know her routine."

"That would work. Something tells me I need to have a look at Cara's place. See if there isn't a clue..." She stopped dead. "She didn't...she didn't say to you she'd found or heard anything?" When he shook his head, she hunted around, then grabbed the paper and pen sitting near the phone, and began to make a list. "Okay, then. We need to get some of Lola's things and bring them back here. Favorite clothes, toys, books, things like that. You need to look into the details of Cara's solicitors and make arrangements to pack up her apartment."

Tears burned her eyes, but this time she refused to let them fall. She'd cried buckets, but life moved on, no matter how much it hurt. Lola and Steve needed closure.

"Jenny?"

She looked over her shoulder to see he'd moved in behind her.

"Have you thought about last night? We need to talk about the personal connection between us."

She grimaced, but he shook his head.

"I've been thinking and have something important I want to ask. A favor if you will." He blinked several times while brushes of scarlet painted his cheeks.

"Steve? What's wrong?"

"We need to talk, but when we're alone. Away from little ears. In the car, maybe?" Then he glanced away, avoiding her gaze.

Her eyes narrowed in recognition he was avoiding something unpalatable. She shrugged. They hardly knew each other, so she supposed it made sense that he felt uncomfortable asking her for a favor. "Okay, in the car."

She brushed off the query, wondering if she'd get a chance to do a little snooping, maybe check out the area or find something tangible to help Lola.

Steve nodded. "Okay, I'll ring Dave now."

He picked up the phone and dialed.

Quickly, he outlined the situation to his friend. "Cara's friend Jenny is staying with me, helping with Lola and sorting through stuff."

It hurt more than she was prepared to admit that he wasn't more open about their relationship, then she mentally kicked herself. What relationship? Friends with benefits? Well, they weren't even technically friends, she reminded herself. He grimaced at something Dave said, and she smiled, refusing to let him see the pain she felt.

In the end, Steve arranged for Dave to arrive within the hour to look after Lola because Fiona would only be available that evening. He smiled and gaily suggested that perhaps he and Jenny should enjoy the break and head out on the town. Whatever his friend said, he laughed tightly and hung up.

"Jenny, I didn't mean—"

She leaned forward as if to kiss him, and then laid a soft finger against his lips. "I understand. Trust me, no one understands better than me." She stood up and walked out of the room.

Dave arrived and they settled the little girl with him then headed for the car in the garage.

Steve had seen the minute he said the words on the phone to his friend that Jenny had taken his words the wrong way. Hell, all he'd wanted to do was protect her. He couldn't even get that right. Frustration ate at him.

She avoided any suggestion that they could have a relationship. She didn't even like herself, for God's sake. He wondered how much of that had been Cara's doing. She'd been sunny, outgoing, but also waspish on occasions. Quick to draw attention to people's shortcomings, and Jenny believed she had more than enough of those.

He really needed to get his shit together.

He ran an unsteady hand through his hair. Jenny's words from earlier also worried him. He agreed that whatever had happened to Lola had taken place near Cara's. While he wanted to resolve Jenny's issues, he wasn't ready to deal with the emotions that roiled within him. Instead he focused on getting them to the apartment in one piece. This was the opportunity to raise his idea.

"Ready?" He waited for her breathy 'yeah' before he turned on the engine. "Good." He leaned over and kissed her on the lips. "Oh, and by the way, you look fantastic in that outfit." He winked and watched her stunned surprise. "Now hang on. I'm half-expecting someone to be waiting for us outside the community."

He pulled out of the garage and they watched the roller door shut as the car reversed onto the street. He drove carefully, watching left and right for anything out of the ordinary, and once they were on the open road, his mind tuned back into the role he'd been so comfortable with before leaving the police force

He suddenly realized that what he'd felt for Cara hadn't been love. It had been passionate and hot, but since meeting Jenny, he wondered if he'd somehow talked himself into the position where he'd imagined it was deeper than it really was. He was confused, because he honestly didn't know how, or even if, he should tell Jenny that. She already felt enough guilt for sleeping with him.

Would his proposition make things worse? He wasn't sure, but when he'd seen the address on that white envelope—the one for Child Services—he knew his time was running out.

"Jenny? What would you say if I said I needed you to stay here and help me keep custody of Lola?"

She turned in the seat. "I'd say tell me what you need me to do."

His breath escaped on a hiss. "There has to be two people and a relationship for me to keep her. Otherwise, they'll send her to a foster home. The envelope on the side was from Child Services. As a single man..." He let the words trail away.

She paled in the seat beside him. "A single man?"

"Yeah, but if I was married or engaged, they'd give me more time, and I could put a case together."

"Married...or engaged?"

Her lips had turned white. For a moment he feared she was about to faint. "Jenny?" "What exactly do you want, Steve?"

"I want us to... If we were engaged, we could make a case. Just to keep Lola, of course."

He wasn't quite lying to her, he temporized. More leaving out some aspects he hadn't yet come to terms with. "Jenny, they're going to take her away. Rip her from the only security she knows. It's not fair to her. Please, will you help me? Will you accept my proposition? We don't have to get married if I can make a case without it."

She flinched. "Whatever you need, Steve."

Deep down in his heart though, he knew he'd taken the wrong tack.

Jenny remained silent for the rest of the long drive, her gaze averted as if she were

thinking something important over. His gut told him he'd just made a major mistake, but by the time they arrived she seemed almost back to her normal self.

He used the keycard Cara had given him to enter the secured parking area, and the large metal grill closed behind him with a ratcheting clang. He pulled into the spot beside Cara's little sports car. She'd loved it, but he'd mentioned to her that a car like that wasn't suitable for carrying a child. She'd grinned and ignored his pointed remark. He frowned at the memory. Was this another aspect of Cara he'd ignored or rewritten in his quest to believe he loved her?

Jenny stepped out of the car as he did the same. She reached for the bag she'd stashed on the back seat. "You have a key?" Her black eyebrow quirked, and he nodded.

"We need to use this elevator." He indicated the one next to the car. "It's the private one to her level." He slipped the keycard through the holder and reached across to take the bag from her as they stepped inside.

"No, it's fine. I need to do this." Her quiet voice was firm, and he let it go, even though he didn't want her to struggle with the weight. She kept a careful, physical distance during the ride to the penthouse.

Cara had always loved the high-life. She'd said it was what she'd been used to with her parents, and he'd understood that sentiment.

Eventually, the ding told him they had reached the correct floor. Without thinking, Steve moved in front of Jenny as the doors slid open. The corridor was empty, and he ushered her forward, digging out the key to the penthouse. The door opened silently, then he stepped inside, casting a quick, assessing glance over the room. It looked exactly as it had when he had last been there, before their final argument. He hadn't been back since.

He closed and locked the door, shooting home the security chain, and then looked at Jenny. "What do you want to do first?"

She looked him in the eyes. "Well, you need to pack up Lola's stuff first, and then I guess it wouldn't hurt to empty the fridge." Her words were calm and measured, and he marveled at her ability to contain herself. "Which way was Cara's bedroom?"

"You've never been here before?" Steve frowned. *Wasn't that unusual?*

"No. I've been in Melbourne for a while. She bought the place after I left." She looked around, checking out the minimalist furnishings, her eyes assessing each piece.

"You aren't a fan of this kind of layout?" He waved a hand across the room, and she shook her head.

"Not really. I mean, it suited Cara. She was at home with this sort of lifestyle, but her parents' place...that was lovely."

"They didn't live like this?"

She answered on a quick burble of laughter. "Oh no! Cara's mum wasn't into flash. They had a nice cottage-style house with comfortable furniture. Nothing ostentatious, just...nice. Rather like them."

Steve frowned again. Not at all as Cara had described it.

"Come on. We should get started." Her tart reminder that time was passing dragged him from his reverie.

"What's your place like?"

She laughed, and he smiled in response. "I think the best way I could describe it is Op Shop Special."

"But with your degree—"

"I may have a degree, but I also have bills. Rent, food, my student fees to pay off, just like everyone else I know." She looked at him. "But that's not why we're here, so show me Cara's room and I can get started."

He nodded and pointed to the door on the other side of the lounge. She smiled and retreated, pushing open the door as he headed for Lola's room. The little girl needed her toys and clothes.

CHAPTER NINE

Jenny entered the bedroom. The pale yellow and pink bedspread matched the curtains.

The carpet was a sunny yellow, and the walls a clean, fresh white. The details of the room made it look like something out of a magazine. Cara had always liked décor like this, but to Jenny's eye, it looked practiced and polished. Not at all like a home.

Jenny moved into the room. The Queen Anne furniture—white and gilt—was probably the real thing, she guessed as she trailed her hand across the dressing table. Cara craved the finest and most expensive, but the room felt strangely soulless. On another level, Jenny felt even more uncomfortable entering a bedroom Steve and Cara had shared, as if she were invading yet another part of Cara's life.

"Don't be silly. You're here to help Steve pack up. This room will be too...emotionally challenging for him." Not true, of course, but the lie made her feel just a little better.

Steve wasn't some fragile male with an ego that needed stroking. She'd already seen his backbone, and that made her want and love him more. Love. The realization stunned her.

"Shit!"

"Everything okay in there?" Steve's voice echoed across the apartment.

She ran her fingers through her hair. "Yep, just dropped something."

Dropped something my foot! *First I sleep with Cara's man then I fall for him. I'm such a horrible friend.* A lump formed in her throat.

It took several minutes before she could find the fortitude to consider what needed doing now. She'd left Cara's bag in the lounge. She'd go and get it in a minute. She moved back to the bed, noting the small bedside drawers, and smiled. Cara had always made sure she had bedside tables to stash her journal and phone...and probably her toys too!

She snorted at the memory of the time Cara's parents had come into the room while Cara was showing Jenny her vibrators. Jenny had cringed with embarrassment. Cara had seen the blush on her mother's face, but laughed gaily. "All the other girls have them, Mum. Right, Jenny?" She'd nudged Jenny in the ribs, and Jenny had nodded, irrespective of what she'd thought.

Jenny opened the bedside drawer, spying her journal. She shouldn't...she knew that, but she picked it up anyway. Maybe there was a clue inside, one no one else had discovered. There had obviously been no search of the unit, maybe because the murder took place in another state. She opened journal to a point approximately midway.

Thursday 13th
What a night. Steve is okay in bed. A little unadventurous,
but I don't mind. Lola is getting on my nerves though. I
suppose I should be grateful that she isn't speaking. But still,
it seems to aggravate Steve that he can't get her to talk to him.
And then I accidentally let slip about poor little Jenny. Good
thing I've been grooming her for a long time. Now I'm going
to have to make out like I'm heading to Melbourne looking

for her help. I mean, like I really want Lola to speak. After
what she saw in the warehouse, if she ever said a word, I'd
have to do something about her. Then I'd have Steve to deal
with.

God, I'm so sick of the charade. Sure, the money is going to be
worthwhile, but it's driving me nuts. It's a good thing I have
Jarvis to keep me satisfied sexually.

Anyway, time and money are two things on my side. And it's
a damn good thing that Steve would never stoop to reading
my journal, so I can tell you everything.

Jenny gasped as she read the entry. Dear God. Cara had been
involved in something right up to her eyeballs. Who the hell was
Jarvis?

Her trembling fingers touched the writing. Disbelief and fury
coursed wildly through her veins. Cara had been using them. All of
them. Including herself. Nausea churned, and she clapped her hand
over her mouth, scrunched up her eyes...anything to relieve the
anguish she felt because of Cara's journal entry.

The moment passed, and she reached out with a shaking hand. I
need to know if there's more. She stuck the small ribbon into the page
then flipped toward the front of the journal.

Tuesday 18th
It's odd. It feels like just yesterday that Jarvis told me it was
done. Who knew getting rid of the oldies would be so liberat-
ing? It's been three years and now the will is finalized, I'm
free to enjoy my inheritance. I can't believe the administra-
tion of the estate was so protracted. The old codger of a
lawyer refused to divide the assets for nine months, and with
all the other delays... Well, it's no matter now. I'm feeling
great!
What's more, little Jenny moved to Melbourne today, and

good riddance! But all the hours I spent in that stinking hospital gave me an alibi that was iron-clad if anyone ever does question where I was. Not that I expect they will now. *No one suspected me of doing anything wrong. After all, the grieving daughter routine was pretty convincing all the way through. Maybe I should pursue a life on screen? On second thought, early mornings and listening to others really doesn't appeal.*

*With Jenny off the scene, Jarvis and I plan to get together in a hotel tonight, somewhere no one knows me. We're going to fuck like bunnies on steroids. I guess I'd better stick to my boring black outfits, but I think I'll surprise him and go commando. I love the feeling of the wind on my bare fanny anyway.*

Jenny's head ached. Oh! How on earth would she tell Steve? He'd be devastated. Anger surged through her as silent tears rolled down her cheeks. How dare Cara use them like this? Even worse was the information that Cara had been involved in the murder of her parents!

The pain and anguish she'd felt evaporated, leaving her with a dose of righteous anger. The bitch! Jenny checked the handwriting; it was definitely Cara's.

She shook her head, assessing the situation as calmly as she could. Poor Lola! Clearly she'd seen something that traumatized her. How could Cara do that to the little girl? It was cruel, but the Cara revealed in the journal was cold and malicious.

No doubt the fright of living with Cara day after day had reinforced the depths of her fear, enduring whatever Cara cooked up. No wonder Lola had clung to herself. Steve would be tainted by association, and Jenny started thinking of ways to offset the damage.

Jenny stared at the journal, revulsion filling her. She wanted to fling the poisonous book from her presence, but knew she needed to show it to Steve. She would need to be there for him too. With the tips of her fingers, she lifted the book, holding it as far away from her as possible, as if just by touching it she'd be tainted. She marched out the door and to the room where the door stood open.

When Jenny reached the doorway, she stilled. She watched him carefully piling clothes into the small suitcase on the bed, ensuring everything was folded neatly. He'd seemed to have found some modicum of inner peace, and she was about to destroy that. Again.

On a deep breath, she entered the room. "Steve? You need to see this."

Her voice wobbled and he turned, frowning. "Are you okay?"

His words warmed her for a second, and then she shook her head, pushing the journal

into his hands.

He took it, but once he realized what it was, he tried to push it back into her hands. "No. I

won't—"

"You need to read it, because the answer is right here."

He frowned, and she grabbed the journal from his grasp, flipped to the page with the

ribbon, and shoved it back to him. She willed him to glance down. After a brief look, his gaze met hers once more.

"What?" There was shock in his voice, and she knew what he'd read. She pointed again and he read further, his face turning white with shock as his lips flattened.

"The bitch. That cold-hearted bitch!" His eyes flashed with anger, and she stepped back.

He dropped the book on Lola's bed. It made a sighing sound as it bounced, and she wondered if it were the pages apologizing for holding such horrific secrets. Her mind scrambled once more for reality in a world rapidly spinning out of control.

"Steve? Do you know someone named Jarvis?"

Steve breathed heavily, and she was sure he was fighting to

contain his rage, then he looked at her. "No, but I'd say it's time we found out who he is and what part he played in this game."

Steve pulled out his phone and called Dave while working to control the shaking of his

hands. "Dave? We found some information you're going to need to see. Can you organize for Fiona to take over looking after Lola now?"

He waited, listened as Dave called Fiona on the home phone and she agreed to head straight over to his place. Steve felt grateful to have such good friends who could help him solve the crime and ensure Lola's safety.

After ringing off, he sat down next to Jenny on the bed. She was gazing at the wall, and he shivered, hoping she wasn't going to somehow find a way to believe it was all her fault. She was hurt, as was he, but he remembered the white marks on her wrists. Faded slash marks. He wouldn't let her backslide after this revelation.

The thought of her bleeding on the floor and thinking it was the only way to deal with the situation terrorized him. How could he live without her now? In a short period of time, she'd become essential to him in ways he couldn't even explain.

What he'd felt for Cara was a dim and faded version of the depths of his need for Jenny. It wasn't just sexual. No, this was the need of a man for a woman, the one he needed by his side forever. This was love.

Whatever it was he'd felt for Cara was lust and fascination, but the depth was all on his part. Even then, it was shallow compared to what he now felt for Jenny. He would have never believed that before, not until he met this woman beside him.

He sighed and slid his arm around her. "Are you okay?"

"Yeah, I'll be fine. What about you?" She turned sad eyes in his direction, and it filled him with a mix of both sadness and wonder.

He pushed back an errant black curl from her face. "I'll be fine. We'll all be fine once this is done."

The idea that Cara had duped them in the cruelest manner made him want to smash a fist into the wall. He felt dirty, used, and most of all, deeply betrayed by her, which was silly, because it occurred to him she'd targeted him the moment she'd laid eyes on him.

He couldn't sit still, so he rose and wrenched the doors of the wardrobe open, taking in Lola's clothes. "I can't..."

Jenny rose and headed for Cara's room without a word, and he followed her. Behind the doors of the wardrobe, hung an array of skirts, dresses, pants, and blouses, along with several pieces of his own clothes. Suddenly he needed to see them, to remind himself of the woman who'd brought them to their knees. Cara had played them for fools, laughing at them. Then she'd left them to grieve, and even left that letter with Jenny. In hindsight, it made so much sense. Of course she'd wanted to be here with them. She'd wanted to feed on their emotions like some emotional vampire!

He caught sight of the few items he'd left here, but it felt as if they mocked him. Steve grabbed the hangers and threw his clothes to the floor.

He stood still, looking at them before reality intruded. He picked the clothes up and replaced them on the hangers. Dave would want to check everything out before he allowed them to recommence searching.

Jenny's hands stilled his actions. "Maybe I should do this. You can go check the kitchen or lounge if it helps." Her quiet voice calmed him.

"I can't believe..." His words hitched.

"You can't believe she duped us? She duped me for years." He felt the whisper of her breath at his shoulder. "We see what we want to because it makes us feel good." She laughed, but the sound carried no mirth. "And being a psychologist, I should have picked it up, but I didn't, because I desperately wanted her to be my friend. I wanted to believe the times she told me that she didn't care I was fat, that I had issues...that I wanted to die."

His heart stuttered in his chest at hearing the words and knowing she had felt that way. He turned and saw the deep pain in her eyes.

"Jenny..." He reached up, framed her face with shaking fingers. "You are beautiful...and I love you."

Her eyes widened, and then she smiled—a genuine smile that lit her eyes. "You know what? I want to believe you. I really do, but..." The grin melted away, and he waited. "I'm not a good judge of character right now. I want to believe you. Give me time." Her eyes conveyed the plea he heard in her voice.

He nodded, a stiff, short movement.

"Perhaps we should check every pocket, every shoe?" She took a backward step and looked around. "She used to love hiding stuff. She was always secretive. It was like a game with her, but it'll be hidden in plain sight. That was her favorite trick."

Jenny reached out to move the clothing aside and he stopped her, speaking quietly. "Not yet, wait for Dave. He won't be far away."

She sighed and walked to the dressing table. "Okay, I'll start here when he arrives. Will you be able to help me with this room, or would you prefer somewhere else?" She looked at him over her shoulder, and he melted.

Here she was, his Jenny, devastated by the level of betrayal, yet worrying about him. She was right, it did hurt, but he needed to do this. Cara had betrayed them both, so he needed to be strong, for all their sakes. Look in the place where they had been intimate and where he'd professed his love. God, she must have been laughing at me the whole damned time!

Now he knew the truth—she hadn't loved him, and what he'd felt was little more than a façade, while his soul waited for Jenny.

"I can do this. We can do this together." He looked at her, and she smiled once more.

He knew the instant the unspoken vow in his words hit home. Her mouth formed a small O.

The doorbell intercom buzzed, and he pinned her with a look. "Stay here, out of sight, until I know it's safe."

She nodded silently.

He padded to the lounge, pressed the video button, and saw Dave and some officers in uniform appear on the screen. "Hang on, and I'll buzz you up."

Within minutes a knock came at the door. Steve looked through the peephole. A knot of people fronted by Dave stood on the other side. He released the air in his lungs, unlatched the chain, and opened the door.

They trooped in and Dave gave him a searching look. "What did you find?"

His stomach curdled for a moment at the thought that Dave would know he'd been taken for a ride. Then he inwardly shrugged his shoulders. It was the only way to catch Jarvis, and he wanted that more badly than anything he had ever wanted before. The only thing he wanted more was to keep Lola and Jenny with him. Forever. The word became a refrain, reminding him of just what was at stake.

"Jenny found it." He motioned for them to follow.

Jenny stood beside the dressing table, watching while he indicated the book on the bed. He picked it up, feeling a shiver of distaste wrack his body.

"Are you okay, man?"

He nodded back to Dave, acknowledging the concern. He opened the book, flicking to the page Jenny had shown him. He watched as Dave read it, his face stony and cold.

"Holy shit!"

Steve smiled, unable to contain his reaction to Dave's epithet. "Yeah, it's a cracker, isn't it?"

Dave turned to Jenny. "Show me where you found it."

She pointed to the open bedside drawer.

"There? Why would she leave it in a bedside table? That doesn't make any sense." Dave had reverted to interrogation mode, and Steve felt the need to protect Jenny, but she smiled. "Because that's what she did. She liked to hide things in plain sight. It was a game with her. One she played even as a child." Jenny took a step forward. "There's more in the journal— lots more. You'll need to read it, but right now, I can tell you she was instrumental in her parents' deaths."

Dave flicked through the book, reading the entries Jenny had marked. "If she was, we'll find the evidence. And this Jarvis...we'll find him and nail him to the wall."

# CHAPTER TEN

Jenny pulled a pale blue dress from the hanger. It was the one Cara had worn in the photo on the bedside table where she was hanging off Steve's arm.

She slumped to the bed, the dress scrunched in her grasp as she gazed at the image on the small table. He was smiling with an enigmatic Lola at his side. Unable to contain herself, Jenny traced her finger over the two of them.

He loved her...or so he believed. She knew he'd been telling the truth as he saw it right now, but she feared it was a reaction to finding out about Cara. God knew she wanted to believe him, because the cold around the region of her heart had warmed when he'd spoken those words.

Did she love him? A flicker in her belly told her there was something, a strong emotion wanting to break free. It could be love, but she'd held herself aloof for so long, any knowledge of that kind of depth now scared her.

"I love Lola." That was easy. The little girl had stolen her heart early on. Steve? That was harder to quantify.

She sighed as she glanced around the room. Steve hadn't yet rejoined her, and she knew he wouldn't press her for a declaration just yet. She bit her lip, knowing she should start going through everything, but the act scared her. The journal had been such a blow. What else would she find?

Jenny rose to hunt through pockets, checking for anything that might contain a clue to where they could find Jarvis.

Dave had asked her to search Cara's bag and she'd done so. They found her phone, turned it on, and scanned the contacts list, but nothing out of the ordinary was in it. They turned it off and bagged it as evidence.

His terse request for her to start on the clothes, to check through everything for cards, SIM cards, or even another phone had been unsurprising. Once he had assured himself she wasn't involved, he'd directed her like the rest of his team to search the apartment. Dave's superior had also made an appearance.

"Detective Skinner, you have new evidence?"

"Yes, sir." Dave handed the captain the journal and indicated the pages to be read.

When he closed the book with a bang, he stared pointedly at Steve.

Jenny wanted to speak out then, but Steve held her still and shook his head as he answered the unspoken question. "No, Captain. At no time did I have even the slightest inkling this was the case."

"Fine. The child?"

"Is safe, with Dave's girlfriend, Fiona, looking after her."

"Good. When we're done, there will be more questions. Stay available." Then the captain had left.

Once more Jenny was angered and sickened by Cara's disregard for human life and emotions.

As Jenny scanned the clothes, she folded them, making neat piles on the bed. Heaven knew what was going to happen to them, but she kept going. A skirt was next, the blue matching the dress that went before. Jenny knew Cara had been proud of her highly organized wardrobe. She'd complained endlessly when her mother had hung things in the wrong place.

After a while, Jenny felt sure there was nothing to be found there. Where could the link be? A spurt of frustration caught her up and she wanted to scream, but she soothed the emotion. She stepped back and scanned the wardrobe, groaning as she realized she'd barely made a dent.

"How's it going?" Steve laid his hands on her shoulders, and she leaned back into his embrace.

"She had a lot of clothes, and this is taking quite a while."

"Yes, she loved shopping." He rubbed lightly, and she felt the muscles in her shoulders relax. "And she always made a show of buying things for Lola and me."

Sounds from the other room filtered through the open doorway as they stood together in a brief moment of silence.

"I can't believe…" He stopped, silent, and she knew what he was feeling. She felt it too. Jenny turned in his embrace, raising her fingers to his cheeks, needing the intimate touch to reassure them both that what they had wasn't the false emotion Cara had invoked in them for such a long time.

"It was a game. We have to remember that…" She stopped as a thought intruded.

He gazed at her, and she felt the shift in his stance. "What is it?" His demand filled the room.

"She liked to buy things for others. Slip stuff into pockets and bags."

He nodded, and understanding dawned across his features.

Jenny turned back to the wardrobe. "Help me get all your things out." She gripped the plastic hangers, tearing at the clothing. "Check to see if anything in the waistbands or cuffs seems off."

Her fingers plunged into a pocket of the jeans she had in her hands. She wiggled her fingers in the soft denim, and there it was—a tiny item hidden where no one would look.

"I think I've found something." She trembled.

"Let me see."

Jenny withdrew her hand from the pocket, the small article gripped in her fingers. It was a SIM card for a phone. "Do you think..."

"It could be." He nodded, not touching it. "Dave! We've found something."

Dave barreled into the room. "What've you got?" His gruff voice demanded an instant answer, and other people crowded the doorway.

Jenny handed him the card. "It was in the jeans in the wardrobe. In Steve's jeans." Dave eyed her, and she glared back. She knew what he was thinking. It was too easy. "She liked to play games, hide stuff in plain sight, particularly when she bought things for someone else."

Dave's eyes flickered uncertainly toward Steve. He nodded his answer, the lines around his mouth white as he ran his hand through his hair. "Yeah, she was big on games. Remember the gift she got Fiona at Christmas? She shoved a gift certificate into the oil burner."

Jenny wanted to sigh. That was a vintage Cara action. She waited for Dave's reaction.

"Right...Simmons?" Dave said to a young female officer who nodded and stepped forward. "Get me her phone."

The woman turned and left the room to return quickly with a bag held between two fingers. "This is what you wanted?"

He nodded, grabbed it, and opened the zipper closure. Fishing out the phone, he sat on the bed and pulled the back and battery from the slim unit. He carefully withdrew the existing SIM and replaced it with the one Jenny had found in the pocket. The room was silent as they all watched Dave replace the battery and back before turning it over.

He glanced up at Steve and then turned it on. The jingle filled the air and the atmosphere in the room was thick. Jenny waited, feeling the turmoil herself. Could this be the beginning of the end? The phone glowed and beeped as messages showed on the machine.

Dave scanned the messages and whooped. "Well done, boys and girls. Jarvis sent her copious messages, with details we can use."

Jenny's legs felt like jelly, and Steve moved in behind her, offering support. Something she hadn't felt so keenly in a long time.

"Dave, I want to collect Lola's stuff and take it home." The rumble of Steve's voice flowed through her system and she shivered. "And I think Jenny and I have done all we can for now."

Dave nodded absently from the bed. "Yeah, grab her stuff. Just...if you find anything, let me know?"

Steve stepped away and she turned, seeing his hand held out to her. She took it, feeling the support and love he radiated. The other police parted to make way for them as they left the room and walked to Lola's.

Considering what they knew, Jenny wondered about the clothes and books. If it were her, she wouldn't want anything tainted by association to Cara, but this was Steve's call.

"Do you really think she'll want all this?" Jenny asked.

Steve stopped. "You're right. Let's leave it all here, except for her photos. We'll take them." He snatched the photos from the pin board opposite the bed.

"Maybe you can arrange for it to be packed up, and when she's ready, she can let you know what she wants to keep."

Steve nodded before he pulled her from the room. "Dave? We're leaving."

Dave emerged from Cara's room. "Going home?"

Steve looked at his watch. "We'll go grab a meal first then head home. Let Fiona know, okay?"

Dave looked at them, as if he were weighing and judging what he saw. Her stomach quivered with nerves, and she bit her lip.

The tension grew thick, and he glanced at Steve then gave a short nod. "Just be careful, okay?"

Jenny grabbed her bag and Steve his keys from the bench where they had left them, then he opened the door and they stepped out of the apartment.

Settled into the car, they merged with traffic.

"Jenny, would you answer some questions?" He needed to know more, to find out what drove this woman at his side.

"Sure, ask away."

Her eyes were closed. He was sure it was the most relaxed she had been since arriving, apart from in their bed. He grinned at that thought. Their bed.

"Why did you go to Melbourne?"

She sighed, and his stomach knotted. "Ah...that's simple. There was a residency program I was able to participate in." She turned and opened her eyes, looking at him. He wrenched his gaze back to the road. "After..." She raised both arms. "After this, not many programs would take me. You have to undergo a psych assessment for the ones I wanted to be involved in. But this one in Melbourne had a special program for those with real-life experience in mental trauma. I fit the bill and was picked from the thirty candidates. So I went."

"What about your family? You never talk about them."

"Oh. They never understood that I couldn't cope as a teenager. It's hard enough being a teen without being...large. I struggled at school and Cara...was my only friend. But looking back, I wonder if it wasn't because she cut me out of the group. I'll have to think about that. But she always seemed to make me feel like I was special. Different, but special. Anyway, once I did this, my parents couldn't cope with my emotional mess. They didn't throw me out, but they just couldn't understand. I wasn't supposed to have problems."

Steve heard the pain and loss in her voice.

"It wasn't a boy?"

She flinched at his question, and he knew he'd struck the final thorn in the wound. "I, uh... There was a boy." She spoke quietly as her fingers twisted in her lap. Steve itched to reach out and unknot them, but he had to know everything. "What happened, Jenny?"

"Do I have to tell you?" There was a wealth of pain in her words, and his heart bled for her.

"I need to know why you keep me at such a distance."

"Distance? I don't think there was much of that in the middle of having sex, do you?" Her fingers flew to her lips, as if trying to shove the words back into her mouth.

"No, but what we had wasn't just sex. So, what happened?"

She groaned. "It was the last year of high school, and I finally got the nerve up to ask this boy to the formal. He agreed, even though I had to really work hard to convince him. He was clever and athletic. You know the kind."

He nodded. He knew the kind exactly.

"Anyway, he picked me up and it was a fantastic night. We doubled with Cara and her date. I was so sure I'd finally found a boy who accepted me for what I was. The real me, with all my lumps and bumps, but he didn't."

"What happened?" The words caught in his throat, nearly strangling him. He thought he knew what she'd say next, but didn't want to hear that she'd been duped.

"We went to the after-party. There was alcohol, and I...stupidly let him talk me into drinking some, then some more. We had sex. The next morning, when I woke up at Cara's, she told me I'd let him strip me off, he'd had me then showed his friends where I'd passed out, naked." She shuddered. "After that, I couldn't face school. The last three weeks were a nightmare."

"But what about your parents?"

"I didn't tell them everything. I couldn't. I was so ashamed of myself and what I'd done. I told them they were teasing me because of my size, which was partly true. They'd started a rumor that I'd almost suffocated Kaden with the rolls of fat."

His fingers fastened around the steering wheel, vise-like. He wished it were Kaden's neck.

"In their eyes, all I had to do was suck it up. Learn to live with my size or slim down. And God knows, I tried...still try."

As he glanced over at her, a single tear tracked down her cheek. His chest burned.

"Maybe...maybe now that I'm here in Queensland, my parents

and I can..." She gulped, and he felt like a heel for making her pain worse. "Maybe we can reconnect again."

"We'll do it together." He growled the words. And by God, if they didn't, he'd keep her safe.

She laughed, a small, wet quaver. "I like the sound of that. Together." She caressed his hand where it sat on the stick shift. "But you can't keep me safe."

He tensed, wondering if he'd somehow telegraphed his thoughts to her.

"I have to live with reality. That's how I cope. One day at a time, one hurdle at a time. It works for me."

"The three of us." That sounded right. Jenny, Lola, and him. Together. "Let's head back to Gino's. It's a weeknight and sure to be empty. We can grab something to eat and talk." Jenny bit her lip again, and he wondered if she could accept his feelings and if she was

ready to do something about it. Steve knew she was raw, inside and out, scraped emotionally by the betrayal.

"Sounds..." She had to clear her throat, her words croaky. "Yeah...sure."

He slid one hand over hers. "Good."

"Will Dave... Will he be able to find Jarvis?"

"There was a number. She must have thought it was safe, because she was using another SIM, though why she wouldn't take it with her is a bit odd."

"Maybe she was meeting him in Melbourne? That would explain why, when she said she was heading down, she had to use me as her alibi. It would also explain why she didn't have the SIM on her."

"You could be onto something there, but I'll leave that to Dave to sort out. I'm not the police anymore."

"How does that make you feel?" The psychologist in her raised its head, and he laughed.

"Fine, I'd actually become a little disenchanted—jaded if you will —by the whole hierarchy thing." He threw her a smile as he pulled into the tiny pizzeria parking lot. "I joined just after my parents died, and I think it was because I felt like I could make a difference in the world that had lost two great people. I was in the car at the time of the accident. Dad lost control. They were killed instantly. I was thrown free, my seatbelt didn't hold me, yet I survived with almost no injuries."

She reached out and touched his hand again. "I'm sorry. That must have been so hard for you."

"It took time to come to terms with it. I know I was living with survivor's guilt for a while after. Now I just miss them." He turned off the engine. "But tonight, I want to focus on you and me, on our relationship, because, before you say anything, that's what we have." He leaned over the console and kissed her softly on the lips.

"All right then, but before we begin our date, ring Dave and tell him what I think. Then we can enjoy our dinner without any other concerns. Oh, and ring Fiona to check on Lola, would you?"

He laughed, the sound carefree for the first time in a very long while, and a smile appeared on her lips. "You already sound like a mother!"

STEVE SETTLED JENNY AT THE TABLE, AND GINO HOVERED anxiously. He'd never really liked

Cara, and in hindsight, Steve understood why. They'd only come here a couple of times, because Cara had groused about the fattening properties of the food.

He could hear her now, the last time they'd visited. But Steve, you know I'm not a big one for lots of carbs. We could have gone to the small Vietnamese place down the road. He'd had to wheedle her to choose something more than a green salad with mineral water. The diamond ring had weighed heavily in his pocket, but it had felt like an ill-starred time to propose.

This time, Jenny smiled broadly and hunted through the choices.

"I really enjoy a traditional lasagna or even involtini di carpaccio. What are you planning?"

It was a refreshing change to be with someone who loved food, so he considered the choices. "All right, I'll order the lasagna and you get the involtini and we can split it."

Gino beamed. "Excellent choice, my friend, and your gorgeous lady should try the Chablis. I imported it for my best customers." With a flourish Gino disappeared behind the curtain.

"Is he always like that?" Jenny reclined in the seat.

"No, only with people he likes. Jenny, I want to..." Before he could finish Gino returned with two glasses and the bottle of wine.

"Let me pour this, then I'll leave you to talk." He winked at Steve who nearly groaned. After Gino finished the task, he sashayed away again.

Jenny giggled. "Oh, that's priceless. Is he expecting you to propose or something?" Steve settled his nerves. "Something like that."

Her eyes widened to large circles. "What?" The word escaped breathlessly between her pink lips.

"I mean...not exactly propose, but I asked you to stay...for Lola. But there's more to this than that."

Shock and surprise flickered over her features. "I'd forgotten the conversation in the car this morning."

"I realize that. But Jenny, I want you to stay. We've got something between us. I love you, and I know you feel it too. I'm not asking for you to tell me you love me. I know you aren't ready for that. We owe it to ourselves, though, to find out what it is. What more is there? I'm asking you to stay. With me."

Liquid gathered at the corner of her eyes, leaving them shimmering in the flickering candlelight. "I've... No one ever cared enough to ask me to stay."

"I do, Jenny. Please?"

He was almost afraid of her answer, but the need to be honest, to keep her here with him drove him on.

"I know you have bills, but—"

"I'm not going to be kept."

He chuckled at the flash of temper and pride. "No, I'm not asking you to. We'll look and find work for you. All I'm asking is that we try and see where this goes."

She gave him a shy, hesitant nod, and his chest ballooned. "Okay, but I'll still need to go back to Melbourne and collect my stuff."

"We'll go together, once this mess is sorted out." She beamed. "Okay."

# CHAPTER ELEVEN

The phone rang as they drove home, both happy but tired after the drama of the day. "Can you answer that?" Steve asked.

Jenny reached down and picked up the phone. "It's Dave." She pressed the button on the phone. "Hi, Dave. It's Jenny. What can I do for you?"

"We've got a line on Jarvis. But it's bad. Really bad."

The crackle of Dave's voice over the hands-free unit had Steve frowning. "Details?" "He's got a criminal record as long as your arm. Assault, GBH, drugs...the list goes on." Silence stretched.

"Background, Dave?"

"Not a lot. Came from Victoria."

"Dammit!" Steve exploded.

"We think he was involved in a couple of heists too. With explosives. He's dangerous and out of jail. We've checked his address, usual haunts, and are hunting down known contacts." "Keep me in the loop." Steve's growl ended the conversation, and the line went dead. "Steve? Does he know where to find Lola? Could it be that she saw whatever happened?" "I'm betting on both."

"But then..."

"Yeah. We need to get home."

Steve accelerated down the highway.

The phone rang again as they drove in the direction of the estate, and Steve had an inkling that it couldn't be good.

"Jenny, hun, answer the phone."

The look she shared with him told Steve that she too felt the presentiment of danger. "Steve's phone." Her words were barely audible.

"Jenny, is Steve there?" Dave asked.

"I'm here."

"Jarvis made it onto the estate. He's...he's holed up inside your house...with Lola and Fi."

The clench in his stomach turned to marble. "How the fuck did that happen?"

"The gate was rammed."

"Jesus." Steve swiped his hand over his brow, dimly noting his hand shook. If Jarvis was somehow behind the mess that had caused Lola's mutism, this would likely damage her further. And he'd left her there, thinking that a gated community, alarm system, and a single adult caring for her would ensure her safety. Anger arced through him.

"Pull over, Steve." Jenny's soft but firm words infiltrated his angry haze.

"We have to get home."

"We do, but you're in no fit state to drive. Getting us home in a hurry is one thing, getting there dead is something else."

"Dammit, Jenny—"

"You're angry, and I understand that, but right now, the last thing that will help her is if you're in the hospital. She needs us once this is done, preferably in one piece. Now let me drive."

"No, I'll drive, but you're right. I need to get control of myself. But Dave?" He didn't know or care how much his friend had heard over the phone. "I'll kill him if I get my hands on him. Understand me?"

"Dammit, Steve, I know how you feel. Fiona is in there too. But I can't let you get involved. You're not on the force anymore." Dave's voice sounded hoarse, and Steve understood the pressure he was under.

"Yeah, right. Just keep me informed."

When the phone clicked off, Jenny covered his hand on the gearstick, gentle and reassuring. "Dave seems like a good man. He'll do everything he can for Lola and Fiona."

The bubble of anger spewed over. "How can you be so damned calm?" The minute the words were out, he regretted them.

Jenny gifted him a sad smile. "I'm not, but right now, I'm holding on to you and the knowledge that there are good people in Lola's corner. It's the best I can do." She pulled her hand away from his and cupped his cheek. "Hope is a strong emotion. It's the one I like best."

He gave a nod, the lump in his throat stopping any chance of talking. She'd humbled him with her quiet words.

When they reached the gates, he saw the flashing lights of the police. The captain waited near the mangled metalwork, and Steve slid the car to a rolling stop.

"Sir?" The officer by the window looked at him, worry and concern etching his face.

When Steve had been at Cara's earlier there had been none of that present, but he knew it was concern for his and Dave's family. He was grateful for it on one level. On another, he felt the primal urge to go in and get Lola and Fiona out.

His muscles bunched and tightened. He pushed on the door, and the captain pushed back. "No, you can't. You're not on the force anymore."

He shoved again, adrenaline coursing through his system. "I'm not going in, I promised Dave, but I need to know what's going on."

The captain sighed and released the door. Jenny clambered out of the other side and huddled up against him. His arm encircled her, hoping to give her some reassurance.

"What's the situation? How is Lola coping?" Steve felt like his mouth had frozen up and Jenny's warmth was the only thing that stopped his heart from seizing with fear.

"We've evacuated most of the surrounding houses. A negotiator has been talking on the phone with him, but it's not looking good. We sent in the SWAT team, and they're in position." "Lola and Fiona?" He placed a soft kiss on Jenny's head when she trembled. He'd never stood on this side of a hostage situation. His appreciation of the strength of those waiting increased.

"We've spoken with Fiona, she and Lola are fine for now. They're in the kitchen. The shooters can see the three of them."

"Your plan?"

"Get them out without loss of life."

THE NIGHT DRAGGED ON. AT SOME POINT, DAVE WAS THERE, shoving a steaming coffee into Jenny's hands. She stared at him blindly.

"Nothing much has happened. You and Steve could go back to my place..."

She shook her head before Dave could say anything further. Steve clearly felt the same with his emphatic, "No."

Dave was tired and drawn. She reached out and grabbed his hand, hoping he'd accept the support. He smiled wanly and settled onto the tiny camp chair beside her.

From time to time, the captain would leave his huddle of advisors and police. Each time they'd look up, hopeful for good news.

"Nothing so far."

The words tore at her, beat her down.

Around dawn there was movement. Jenny lifted her weary head. "What's going on?" Steve and Dave both rose as the captain neared, his face grave.

"Jarvis has ceased communications. I don't—"

A sound rang out, loud and shocking, and her heart stopped thudding in her chest. Men in

Kevlar jackets and protective headgear ran through the gate in the direction of the house. She rose, legs unsteady, and Steve reached out. His hands were chilled, and the worse outcome flashed through her mind. Nausea, caustic and hot, rose in her throat. She fought it back. Stay calm for Steve.

Time was suspended while they waited. She watched the movement, but was now unable to move. Pain lanced through her. Lola?

Steve squeezed her hand. He threaded his fingers through hers, as if he understood her fears.

Dear God. Let her be okay. Let them both be okay. Her stomach churned, and time moved slowly. Cold invaded her body.

Why didn't someone tell them what was going on? Surely by now they knew? She gulped as bile rose again.

The phone in the captain's hand buzzed, and she heard him answer it. He turned away, cutting them off from the proceedings. She stared at his stiff back, her fingers gripping Steve's.

The captain turned, slowly, and for a moment, she feared what he was about to say, until she saw the smile on his face...tired, but triumphant.

"They're fine. They're okay."

She breathed, gulping air. She's alive. She's fine.

Steve shuddered beside her, and she threw herself into his arms, laughing and crying. "She's okay, Jenny," Steve's voice reassured her as he dotted kisses in her hair.

Tears dripped down her face, but she didn't care who saw them. She rose up on tiptoe and kissed him on the lips.

She finally knew the truth. This man...this was the one she'd love until she died, and she didn't care who knew it.

STEVE WAS THROUGH THE GATE BEFORE JENNY, SCOOPING UP

Lola, who cried silently in his arms. "It's okay, Lola. Jenny and I are here. We won't ever let anyone hurt you again."

The child shuddered in his and Jenny's embrace. "You bet. Lola, we love you so much." "Besides which, Jenny promised to stay with us. She's not leaving...ever."

Lola's head popped up, tear tracks making their way down her face. She glanced in Jenny's direction and held out her arms.

Jenny snuggled the girl close, and he smiled. The sight was the best thing he could ever hope for.

"Steve's right." Her smile was radiant as she kissed Lola's cheek, and the little girl

touched hers before she gripped on to Jenny's shoulders. "I can't leave the people I love most in life behind, so you're kind of stuck with me."

"You mean it?" The slow thud of his heart in his chest sped up.

"Yeah, I mean it." She gazed into his eyes and kissed him. "You're stuck with me." Then Jenny laughed gaily.

The captain smiled at them. "We'll need to talk to you later."

"Sure, but right now, we're going to find a hotel and get some sleep." He ushered his family to the car. His family...Steve thought he could get used to that.

EPILOGUE

Steve watched as Jenny crawled onto the bed with a smile. His plan was ready and in place. Two small boxes sat in the top drawer of his bedside table. One designed to give her a night of pleasure, the other to cement the life he wanted them to share. His fingers itched to reach for the second, but he controlled himself. Not yet. Set the scene. She deserves no less.

He looked around, taking in the cool, light green wall opposite the bed. It was a far cry from the cappuccino of the other house, but they'd chosen the house and décor together, with the view to the three of them living there for a long time.

The sound of the ocean crashing soothed the ragged emotions in his chest. He'd planned tonight for the last few days, anxious to ensure they were both relaxed and mellow.

"You're thinking again, Steve." Jenny spoke quietly as she settled on top of the covers beside him.

"Only about how beautiful you are, and how much better my life has become since you entered it."

It was true. Barely three months ago, he'd thought himself in love with Cara and was willing to settle for second best. Then Cara had died and he'd thought his world had ended. He supposed on one level it had, but the real and happy life had begun when he'd met the sad-eyed Jenny at the airport.

In the weeks since they had closed the case on Cara's death and the close shave for Lola and Fiona, they'd decided the best course of action was to move. So the three of them had flicked through house brochures, Lola picking ones she liked. He'd laughingly told her she was intent on picking one with a pool and room for a puppy. She smiled and nodded her agreement.

Jenny looked for one in a good neighborhood, with a school for Lola and lots of children. "She needs to mix more."

Steve had worried about her, given she didn't speak, but Jenny had hunted for a psychologist she felt Lola would click with.

It hadn't been an easy transition for any of them. Lola had suffered wild nightmares for the first two weeks after the siege, and Jenny had been insistent that whenever they had to visit his old house that she not be there with them. He'd found a hotel with a large suite and two bedrooms, which he'd requested so he could maintain his privacy with Jenny, but with Lola only seconds away.

The house by the beach had been perfect. It had a large yard and a fenced pool, so Lola was enchanted. Hell, he'd even promised her a puppy once she was settled. Jenny had fallen in love with the views the balconies afforded and the five bedrooms.

He'd teased her about filling them and she'd blushed rosy red. He hoped they'd fill another bedroom soon.

This morning over breakfast, Lola had uttered her first words. The scene had nearly unmanned him, and he'd had to fight back tears. Jenny had simply enfolded the little girl in her arms. The simple "I love you" from Lola had meant so much.

It seemed appropriate that he propose on the night that the file on Jarvis Mellor and Cara was closed. It had been an exhausting and emotional day, but they'd survived the testimony of those who offered the information that filled in the gaps.

When the coroner closed the case, both he and Jenny had heaved a sigh of relief. "I'm glad that's over, but I'm still amazed they managed to work out where Cara had met Jarvis Mellor." Jenny fluffed up her pillows before settling down with her arms folded over her stomach. "I thought I knew everything there was to know about Cara. Now that we know she met him all those years ago and kept it quiet, I'm surprised." She shrugged. "But then, I guess the Cara we knew was only a front."

"I know. If the Victorian Police hadn't come to the party, sharing the details of the joint Victorian-Thai investigation into Cara's parents' death, we would never have known he was a suspect." He gathered Jenny against him.

"Or that she'd even been interviewed." Jenny snuggled into his embrace, her head on his chest. "At least we know what happened to Lola. I still can't believe Cara had her parents murdered. It still seems like an awful dream."

He shook his head. "And for Lola to have witnessed it. You were the first person to pick up on that."

She twiddled the watch on her wrist. "I think the worst thing was hearing that Cara and Jarvis were involved in trafficking the drugs. Her parents were good people. They didn't deserve to die. Same as Lola's parents."

"No. Even if they were mules for Jarvis and Cara, no one should be tortured and shot. And to have Lola watch, is something I will never forgive Cara for."

"Shh...at least we can do something for Lola. Make her feel better about her memories.

Thank you for arranging for her parents to be interred at the local cemetery. It'll be good for her to be able to visit their gravesite. It will help her, once she's older, to have a positive memory of them."

"Even with what they did?"

"That makes it even more important, Steve."

"Hmm."

"Now tell me what was in the letter that arrived today."

He grinned. "It was from Child Services."

Jenny sat bolt upright in the bed. "What? Why didn't you tell me?" She swung around, her black hair flying like silk.

"They're granting us temporary custody while we work through the formal adoption process."

"Yes!" She fisted the air. "We need to tell Lola."

He gathered Jenny close and kissed her. When she was breathless, he pulled away.

"We'll tell her tomorrow." Steve stroked her hair. "I don't want to talk about that anymore." He snuggled Jenny down again, close against his heart. Now...he needed to ask now. "But what I do want..." He gulped nervously and pulled her face up to his, anxious to gain her commitment. "I need..."

Drawing away slightly, he opened the drawer with one hand and fished around for the box with the velvet finish. His fingers found it and curled around it. He sucked in a deep breath, dropping the box out of sight as he clasped her close.

"Jenny...you know how I feel about you. I tried to show you, tell you, but I want to...I want to ask you to marry me." He finished the words in a rush, his stomach coiling and turning like a nest of snakes. "Please?"

She stilled in his arms, and his chest tightened.

Would she say yes? Would she say no?

She pulled away and gazed into his eyes. "Why are you asking me now?"

Confusion set in. "What do you mean?"

She smiled, just a little uptick of her lips. "Why are you asking me now? Today? Why not yesterday or tomorrow?"

He leaned back, sure there was something deep in the question. "Because today we're starting a new life. I want...no, I need you to be part of it, with Lola and I."

She relaxed and smiled at him, her eyes glowing in the light of the lamps. "Yes, I will, because I love you too."

His heart thumped against his chest. Now he had everything. She loved him, and she was committed to them and their family.

Jenny's heart filled with love. "You know it won't be easy? I'll have good days and bad ones. So will Lola. We're both going to be fairly high maintenance."

He pulled her closer. "If it's worth having, then you have to put in the effort. I'm more than willing to do that for this."

She melted against him, knowing that she too would do everything in her power to make

this relationship work. Steve looked at her steadily as he brought forward a shaking hand, holding a box.

Her breath caught in her throat. "What?"

Steve smiled at her. "This is for you. I hope you like it. If you don't..." His voice trailed away as he opened the box.

Nestled within the satin bed lay the most exquisite emerald and diamond ring, and she wanted to reach out and touch it. To make sure it was real and not some fevered dream. The stones glittered in the light, and she felt her throat clog with tears of happiness.

He lifted the ring, and she carefully extended her hand. His touch feather light, he slipped it onto her finger while her stomach jittered like the wings of a million butterflies. Steve kissed the knuckle of her finger and raised his head.

Steve loved her. Every day he let her know he loved her curves and the softness of her body. His kisses and his touches as he worshiped her body were honest, and she gloried in them.

"So what are you waiting for, lover boy?"

# INHERITANCE OF THE BLOOD BY IMOGENE NIX

***In the darkness evil waits…***

As a young bride Kira was whisked away from everything and everyone she knew, including her new husband and became Christina, an operative of the Displaced Persons Unit.

As the danger grows she sees an opportunity to save her husband

Vasya and sister Serina. But nothing is the same. Serina is grown up—married and pregnant.

Vasya too is older and darkly forbidding. Trusting Christina doesn't come easily until a catastrophic event takes place. Now, knowing the truth everything he thought he knew is changed. But at a very high cost.

The four must work together to defeat the Demon, Zuor and the stakes are higher than they imagined and all could be lost.

--------------------------------------

*The burning at the back of her neck warned she was being watched. A quick glance didn't clarify it. Instead, she turned around in time to see her mother's face, pale. "Mama?"*

*She took a step forward, but her grandfather snatched her wrist.*

*The grip was painful, and Kira stilled. "Let your parents talk."*

*She didn't know what the topic of conversation was, but it couldn't be good.*

*The dappled sunlight seemed cooler than before.*

*Her father crooked his forefinger at her grandfather while they stood there. For a moment she wished Vasya had come with them, but he had to work. Just the thought of her new husband warmed Kira.*

*She only had a few minutes to contemplate her newly defined status as a married woman, when her grandfather pulled at her hand. "Come with me." He tugged and, confused, Kira allowed herself to be towed away.*

*A glance at her parents' faces stole any feeling of well-being.*

*"Grandfather?"*

*"Shh, my love. You must go." His grip was implacable and his face stern, but he shivered.*

*"What are you doing? Where are you taking me, Grandfather?"*

*They moved rapidly through the village they'd visited to sell their wares just that morning, and for the first time since they'd arrived in the market place she felt fear. What was wrong? Was it something to do with Vasya?*

*"You are in danger. We must send you away." The words confused her further. Send her away? Danger?*

*"Where is Vasya?" She stumbled over a stone, but he kept tugging her onwards.*

*With a quick glance around, he hauled her into a dirty laneway between the buildings. Kira gasped, trying to drag air into her starving lungs. "There's no time. We must get you away."*

*A nondescript shopfront lay ahead, and he pushed on the door. It rattled and opened with a loud groan. "Andre? Andre, are you here?"*

*An older man shuffled into the room, bent nearly double from the weight of the load on his back. "Marat? What do you want?"*

*"My granddaughter. They are coming for her and us. Get her away. Take her now, while you can."*

*The man's face clouded over. "Are you sure?"*

*"Grandfather, where is Vasya?" Fright had the blood in her veins pounding.*

*"Hush, my precious. Andre will see you well." He turned. "Whatever it takes, Andre. Take her now." With surprising speed, her grandfather whirled and was gone.*

*The man, Andre, eyed her. "Come this way, child. There is no time to be lost."*

*Eleven years later*

The tattoo of her heart and cry of terror woke her, as they usually did. Once again, as she had since that rapid flight from those who sought her, she found herself in a lonely bed. Hundreds of miles away from everything she'd dreamed of, in a house she'd built for them to share. As always, it left her wishing that Vasya had fled with her.

Instead, here she was, exiled without her husband. With a sob, she rolled over and let the tears fall.

Available from Beachwalk Press
**books2read.com/IOTB**

Direct Autographed Copy
http://bit.ly/2w6g4K6

When Cupid—otherwise known as Diocail— is banished from his home on a remote Scottish Island, he's set a series of tasks by the great god Lugh, who also happens to be his father.

In **Blame The Wine**, he must bring two lovers together... BBW Cara and James, the man she's lusted over from afar who happens to be a super geek and head Veha Industries.

In **A Stranger's Embrace**, Diocail is driven to help an

emotionally fragile Jane and Davis, a famous author. The task is more complicated, with the existence of Carstairs her could-be ex-husband and teenage daughter, Frannie.

In **Revenge on Cupid**, Diocail must take the ultimate chance and find his own happily ever after with Simone. Sometimes the past gets in the way and HEA's don't come cheap though.

---

The dusty, dingy little diner was full, even with its current state of cleanliness—or lack thereof. People from the surrounding offices didn't care about anything except the incredible, well-prepared food at a reasonable cost. They flooded in, like waves to the shore. As one tide left, another swept in.

"Honestly, Simone. I'm going to try getting his attention one more time. If that doesn't work, I'm out of there. I mean, how long can I keep trying?" Cara picked at the caramel tart she hadn't been able to resist with the cheap metal fork and flicked the blob of fresh cream that sat on top to the side of the plate.

"You've said that tons of times before. Besides, what are you going to do to get his attention? Hmm? Walk naked through the typing pool?" Simone bobbed the straw in her smoothie as she eyed her friend with a frown. "It's been what? Eighteen months since you saw him, and you've mooned over him from a distance ever since you met him. You need to move on, Cara. That is, unless there's something you haven't shared?"

The query was arch. Cara shivered even as she shook her head. "No."

Simone quirked an eyebrow, obviously unconvinced with the answer. Cara let out a deep sigh of frustration. "There's a position...it's only temporary, for a PA reporting directly to him." She speared a forkful of tart, chewed quickly and swallowed, before continuing. "In his office, full-time for the period of the engagement. I saw the memo yesterday. I mean, I have the skills, right? I can type, answer phones, make coffee, file, greet people. What's more, I can probably do it better than all those size eights in the typing pool that

Ms. Jackman seems to prefer." She nodded thoughtfully. "All I have to do is get past the ogre in Human Resources."

Simone stared at her, disbelief clear on her face. "Girl, I so remember that woman. If you think you can get past her, you're doing better than I ever did. That's why I left Veha Industries, remember? Maybe it's time to haul out your resumé and consider some other options. Look for something better." Simone shook her head and billows of her crimson hair swirled through the still air.

Cara understood Simone only had her best interests at heart. But this time she knew the outcome would be different. Hell, she could feel it in the air. The tingle of expectation.

"Cara, the HR ogre will hang you out for breakfast before she offers you anything like a position in that office. Remember her mantra? Good looks and good work make for a positive workplace!"

Simone didn't sugar-coat anything. It was another great reason for their long- term friendship. Honesty. But Cara didn't want to hear the truth in the statement. Even if it was exactly as her friend said.

Cara nodded quickly. "Yeah, I know, but if I don't try, then I won't know how close I can get to him, right? And the only way to catch his attention is to get past *her* and see him in person." Cara quaked a little at the information she needed to share. The favor she needed to ask. "Anyway, I tidied up my resumé and dropped the application into a memo envelope yesterday, so it's too late to back out now. I mean, fortune favors the brave. Doesn't it? If I don't snag an interview, I'm going to visit the career advisor across the street and register with them." She shrugged. "I'll look for temp work until something more long-term shows up. I can see what they have on offer and well...who knows? Maybe a job with the right boss is just waiting for me. But I'd rather this worked out, to be honest." Her voice trailed off into a whisper. "I really wish he would notice me."

Simone took a long slurp of her banana drink, and Cara noticed her questioning gaze even as she squirmed. Finally, Simone nodded. "It's your funeral. So anyway, you'd better show me this memo if you want me to be a referee for you. I'm guessing that's what you need, right? I'll have to know what I'm supposed to say about you before they ring."

Cara smiled. "Thanks, Simone. I knew I could count on you." She slipped a piece of paper out of her handbag and handed it over. "Sorry it's a bit creased. It was in the bottom of my bag, I stashed it so none of the others from the pool would see. You know how it is."

Available from Love Books Publishing
**books2read.com/CelticCupid**

Direct Autographed Copy
http://bit.ly/2vs7wtS

# BIOCYBE BY IMOGENE NIX

*Can a cyber-enhanced warrior and a ship's captain find love together?*

Levia Endrado never wanted to be a warrior, but at seventeen she was deemed suitable for battle. After intense training and multiple enhancements, which gave her superior strength and healing ability, she was sent off to defeat the enemy—a killing machine with a mission.

When the war was over, she had to find a new life. At twenty-seven she's a washed-up veteran without a future. Or she was, until she met Sandon Daria.

Serving as a pilot aboard Sandon's spaceship the *Golden Echo* makes Levia long for a different and gentler life. But old hurts and even older enemies aren't so easily forgotten. Particularly when they come back for her.

Sandon is determined to show Levia that she's more than just a BioCybe...she's the woman who completes him. Getting close is just the first step, keeping her alive is an even bigger challenge, but one he's willing to take because the prize is their combined future.

----------------------------------

Levia scanned the long line of other hopefuls entering the chamber. The large building in the center of town was cold, and she dragged her wrap around her body, even as she craned her head, looking to the high ceiling. She'd never before had an occasion to enter the testing complex, yet she'd seen the lines of teenagers every time they passed the building.

Once she'd asked her parents why the teens were lined up and her mother's face had shuttered. Her stepfather had just shaken his head and growled. They'd stopped her questions with a carefully uttered, "You'll know soon enough, Levia." The pain in her mother's eyes had been enough to shush her questions. For endless months afterward, her parents had traveled different routes to the educational facility she attended and Levia lost interest in the puzzle of that building.

Now, as she looked around, remembering that long ago spring day, it was her opportunity to find out. But she felt a surge of concern at what lay ahead. She likely wasn't the only one, given that there were probably two to three hundred seventeen-year-olds gathered in the one place. Ahead of her, she caught sight of a couple of girls, their arms linked together and wide smiles on their faces. Scanning the crowd, she became aware that, by far, a majority of those gathered displayed both fear and trepidation.

"All female subjects will enter through doors three, six, and seven. All male subjects will enter through gates four, eight, and ten." The speaker above her was loud, and she jumped before checking the numbers etched on the black metal sign over her head.

The massive doors beside her swung open, and now an uncertain silence reigned. Many of the youngsters hung back, clearly discomforted by whatever testing regime lay ahead. This was where they'd been told their futures would be determined.

"Oh gosh, I hope they only have an aptitude and psych eval. I don't think..." Levia turned to see the white face of the girl behind her. The girl had uttered what many must silently be thinking.

Levia dragged an unsteady breath in, her hand resting flat against the plane of her belly as she looked around. No one had entered yet. It was clear many were on the verge of taking the step, but still they hung back.

She straightened her shoulders. "I'm not afraid." It was always wiser to approach things head-on, she believed. When her biological father had died, she'd been one of the few to view his capsule before it was sent into the massive gray structure built to accommodate those who'd moved onto the next life realm.

Her legs shook as she wobbled toward the entrance. Beyond the doorway, she spied sealed cubicles and her heart stuttered. Why cubicles? Usually testing—med and psych—were in eval-units, hidden only by billowing white curtains. She glanced back, noting that others had taken the first step.

"Move along, subjects." Once again, the androgynous voice of the address system blared.

Of course, given it was her seventeenth anniversary of birth, she was technically considered an adult now.

She thought longingly of baby Rald and her half-sister, Elda, waiting at home for her to return, and the celebrations to be held that night. That made her smile. She would need to make them proud of her.

She entered a row and the tall Educational Specialist, the edu-specs as her peers laughingly called them, stopped her. "Present your credentials to the scanner."

She'd done this many times since the tiny implant had been slipped below the dermal layer of her skin at birth. The small unit in her wrist heated as her details were checked.

"Enter the first cubicle, Levia Endrado, and follow the instructions to complete your assessment."

Thus dismissed, Levia moved to the first unit, laid her palm against the scanner, and the door slid open soundlessly.

"Welcome, Levia Endrado. Take your place in the eval-unit." The soft contralto of the voice echoed after the door closed silently behind her.

"What are you evaluating?" Her voice was breathy, and she peered around.

"Your skills—physical and psychological. Your emotional and medical status. Your educational attainment levels."

It was an answer that shed little insight into the many things she was hungry to know. "Why do all seventeen year olds—"

"Take a seat, Levia. Then we may begin your testing."

If she'd expected an answer, she was sadly mistaken, she considered sourly. She dropped into the seat, the soft leather-like surface molding to her body.

"Levia Endrado, you are required to remove all non-specified apparel."

She jolted in the chair. "It's cold."

"The temperature will be amended. Remove the non-specified apparel."

Her misgivings grew as she dragged off the light wrap she'd brought with her, and then threw it to the floor at the side of the unit.

"We will begin, Levia Endrado. At any time, should you experience any malfunctions of the unit, simply depress the red button." It glowed and she grimaced.

Levia reclined against the chair and waited for the testing to begin.

The first examination was based on her understanding of the political system, where she saw herself, and her knowledge of the rights and responsibilities accorded through citizenship of both her planet and the commonwealth.

The second test was mathematical and scientific proficiency. It felt like hours had passed by the time she'd finished, and she lay limp on the seat, exhausted.

"Levia Endrado, you may rise. The sanitary unit will emerge once you trigger the yellow button at the door. Should you require refreshment, press the blue button and a restorative will be made available."

"Can I leave?"

"Negative, Levia Endrado. Your needs will be catered for in this capsule."

"Why?" Her voice hitched and true fear rose for the first time. Why did they keep her in the alcove?

"All will be revealed at the end of the testing cycle."

Levia looked at the now empty screen before hurling a curse word. It was met with silence.

The urgent throb of her bladder reminded her that she needed to use the facilities, so, with

a sigh, she rose and clambered from the seat. After attending to the needs of her body, she walked around the unit, peering at the door, but it was obviously programmed remotely. She poked and prodded, but it made no difference. With a huff, she headed back to the chair.

The moment she'd settled in, the viewing screen shone bright. "Welcome back, Levia. The next sequence will evaluate your psychological reflexes, then that will be followed up with the general knowledge portion of the evaluation."

"When can I leave?" It seemed better to ask bluntly, she told herself.

"Once the examination is completed. After the next set of evaluations, you will be subjected to the physical aspect."

"Then I can go home?"

"Levia Endrado, you will now complete the psychological test. This will be undertaken by one of the center's personal evaluators."

She frowned. Personal evaluators? She bit her lip, and the sting reminded her that this wasn't something to joke about. In her seventeen years, she'd only heard of personal evaluators being brought in once before, and that was when one of the girls at her academy had been in a serious accident. Both legs were amputated and her body's ability to keep her alive had been gravely compromised. Her peers had been informed that the girl had requested the assessment before she could request her support systems be disconnected.

"Levia Endrado, are you ready to recommence processing?" The emotionless voice echoed once more and she gulped.

"Yes."

Available from Beachwalk Press
http://www.beachwalkpress.com

Direct Autographed Books
http://bit.ly/BioCybe

# ALSO BY IMOGENE NIX

### **Warriors of the Elector**

- Star of Ishtar
- Starline
- Starfire
- Star of the Fleet
- Starburst
- The Star of Eternity

The Star of Ishtar & Starline - Print

Starfire & Star of the Fleet - Print

Starburst & The Star of Eternity - Print

### **Blood Secrets (Re-releasing 2020)**

- The Blood Bride
- The Illuminated Witch
- The Sorcerer's Touch

### **The Search Duology**

- Miss Elspeth's Desire
- Miss Isabelle's Craving (Not Yet Released)

### **Reunion Trilogy**

- War's End
- The Assassin
- Executing Justice

The Reunion Trilogy in Paperback

## Sex Love & Aliens

- Tangled Webs
- False Webs
- Covert Webs

## 21st Testing Protocol

- Cyborg: Redux
- Children Of A Greater Evil (Not Yet Released)
- When Evil Came To Stay (Not Yet Released)
- Finis: The War To End All Wars (Not Yet Released)

## Celtic Cupid Trilogy

- Blame The Wine
- A Stranger's Embrace
- Revenge On Cupid

The Celtic Cupid Trilogy in Paperback (August 2019)

## Zombieology

- The Reset (2018)
- I Dream of Zombies (2019)
- The Six Million Dollar Zombie (Not Yet Released)

## Knights of Pleasure

- Silken Knights (Not Yet Released)

## Single Titles

The Chocolate Affair

Falling In Love Again (Previously A Sapphire For Karina)

BioCybe

Hesparia's Tears

Tomorrow's Promise

A Bar In Paris (also coming to paperback)

Inheritance Of The Blood

The Plan

Loving Memories (also coming to paperback)

Hero of Heartbreak Hill

Raspberry Dreams (Not Yet Released)

## Non Fiction

Self Publishing: Absolute Beginners Guide (With Suzi Love)

## Written as Ciara Cave

25 Curated Ways To Get Rid Of Telemarketers

Book Signings for Absolute Beginners

# ABOUT THE AUTHOR

Imogene is published in a range of romance genres including Paranormal, Science Fiction and Contemporary. She is mainly published in the UK and USA.

In 2010, Imogene Nix (the pen name not Imogene herself) was born. Imogene sat down and worked tirelessly for 3 months culminating in the book Starline, which became the first in a trilogy titled, "Warriors of the Elector." Since then she's had over 30 titles published and is now focusing on hybridising herself - with a mixture of traditionally published and self-published works.

In fact, she's taking control of many of her back catalogue books, which are slowly re-releasing as self-published titles.

Imogene is a member of a range of professional organisations world wide, and believes in the mantra of mentoring and paying it forward and is actively involved in mentorship (through NaNoWrimo and her vlog: In The Chair With Imogene Nix) and tutoring of new and upcoming authors.

In her spare time she loves to drink coffee, wine & eat chocolate and is parenting her spoiled dog and a ferocious cat along with her husband and 2 human daughters and looks forward to weekends away with her husband in their caravan "The Seven Year Hitch!" Do look forward to her caravan romance at some point!

*To Contact Imogene*
www.imogenenix.net
imogene@imogenenix.net

facebook.com/ImogeneNix

twitter.com/ImogeneNix

instagram.com/ImogeneNix

www.ingramcontent.com/pod-product-compliance
Lightning Source LLC
Chambersburg PA
CBHW071526100726
47908CB00004B/1306